LITTLE HIDDEN FEARS

GEORGIANA GERMAINE SERIES
BOOK 11

CHERYL BRADSHAW

LITTLE HIDDEN FEARS

Georgiana Germaine Series, #11

By *New York Times & USA Today*
Bestselling Author

CHERYL BRADSHAW

This book is a work of fiction. Names, characters, places, businesses, and incidents either are the products of the author's imagination or are used in a fictitious manner. Any similarity to events or locales or persons, living or dead, is entirely coincidental.

"Courage is not the absence of fear. It is going forward with the face of fear."

Abraham Lincoln

CHAPTER 1

Noelle Winters slipped in between the guests, humming to herself as she scooped up a few empty plates off the table and walked to the kitchen. Handing them off to one of the staff members she'd hired to assist her for the evening, she moved a hand to her hip, reminiscing over the night's events.

The party was winding down now, a fact she was pleased about. Over the last hour, her feet had begun to hurt, making her wish she hadn't worn heels in the first place. She wanted nothing more than to kick them off and go barefoot for the remainder of the evening. And given most of the remaining attendees were at least a few wines in, she doubted anyone would notice, or care, for that matter.

Six months of party planning had all come down to tonight, throwing the perfect engagement party for Zoey, her best friend since grade school. It was hard to believe a year ago Zoey was single and had announced she'd sworn off men for life. Noelle hadn't believed a word of it. And sure enough, Zoey retracted the statement the second she laid eyes on the debonair Lucas Bronson.

After a whirlwind, three-month romance, Lucas proposed,

and Zoey said yes. Over the next several months, they planned their wedding. In a few short weeks, they'd marry, move in together, and begin their new life in Cambria, California."

Thinking about it now, it was hard for Noelle to believe how much had changed in so little time.

But Zoey was happy, which was all Noelle had ever wanted.

And while she was excited for the next chapter in Zoey's life, there was a looming sense of unease in her own. In recent days, she'd taken an unexpected risk, one she might not have taken, even though it was the right thing to do. But that was a tomorrow problem. Tonight was about Zoey.

A hand brushed across Noelle's arm, and she turned to see a beaming Zoey standing next to her in a satin, champagne-colored, split-thigh dress. She recalled the day they'd gone shopping for it. Zoey must have tried on at least fifty dresses that day. But when she stepped out of the dressing room in the one she wore now, they both knew their search had ended.

"I can't thank you enough for hosting my engagement party," Zoey said. "Every single moment tonight has been amazing."

Noelle smiled, saying, "If you're happy, I'm happy."

"I am. Hey, I haven't seen Lucas for a while. Have you?"

Noelle hadn't.

She'd been so focused on the party there hadn't been much time to focus on anything else.

"Sorry, no. I've been preoccupied," Noelle said.

Zoey draped an arm around Noelle's neck. "I thought that's why you hired staff tonight, so you could relax and enjoy the party along with everyone else."

"I know, I know. I can't help it. I want everything to be perfect."

"It *is* perfect. Promise me you'll relax now."

"I promise I'll try."

"Where's Kiera? I haven't seen her much tonight either."

"Dominic took her up to bed about a half an hour ago. I bet he's still with her, helping her settle in," Noelle said.

"Or hiding out somewhere upstairs. Your husband has never been comfortable in a room full of people."

Noelle shot Zoey a wink. "That's true, but when I suggested hosting the party here tonight, he was a good sport. I'm surprised he lasted as long as he did."

"I'm not. He'd do anything for you."

Almost anything.

"It's just about time for the toast," Noelle said. "And given the guests have gone through almost all of the champagne, I need to bring in some reinforcements."

"Should I send someone to get more bottles?"

"Not only do I have backups, I have backups for the backups."

They both laughed, and Noelle excused herself, heading upstairs to grab the additional bottles of champagne she'd stashed in the wine fridge upstairs. Along the way, she cracked open her daughter's door and peeked inside. Five-year-old Kiera was curled on her side, fast asleep, her favorite white teddy bear clutched in her arms. Dominic was nowhere in sight.

Noelle pulled the bedroom door closed and rounded the corner. She made her way to the wine fridge and bent down. The moment she reached inside to grab the bottles, the lights went out, cloaking the room in darkness.

She heard gasps and cries of surprise from the guests downstairs as they bumped around, trying to find their way in the dark. Noelle thought she'd considered every possible scenario for tonight, but losing power had been the furthest thing from her mind.

Thoughts swirling, she searched for a solution … and then, clarity came. Each of the skinny, high-top tables she'd rented for the evening had been decorated with a candle in its center. All she needed was to grab the mini flashlight out of her desk drawer, locate the matches in the kitchen, and light the candles.

She stood and reached out, using her hands to feel her way along the wall toward her office. The moment she stepped inside, a strange sensation gripped her, like someone's hands around her neck. And then came the squeeze, a crushing pain unlike anything she'd ever felt before.

Noelle wrestled for breath, but breath didn't come, and as she struggled to maintain consciousness, every little hidden fear she'd ever had came collapsing down around her.

CHAPTER 2
TWO WEEKS LATER

I was sitting at my desk at the detective agency, waiting for my next appointment to walk through the door. The woman was late. Seventeen minutes late, to be precise, and given I was a stickler for timeliness, I had a notion to cancel the meeting altogether.

Another eight minutes ticked by, and I decided to do just that. Then the front door opened.

A disheveled woman with long, auburn hair, the likes of which looked like it had been through a windstorm walked in. Her boho attire included a pair of colorful striped leggings, a light blue, floral print, V-neck blouse, and brown, suede booties.

She grabbed a ponytail holder off her wrist, pulling her hair back into a loose bun.

"Are you Zoey Morgan?" I asked.

"I am."

"You're twenty-five minutes late," I said.

She looked at me, blowing out a burst of air, and shrugged. "I am so sorry. I could have sworn I set my alarm last night, but this morning, it didn't go off. I hope you're not too upset with me."

I was, but saying as much wouldn't change a thing.

"Take a seat," I said.

"Oh, yes, thank you."

As she lowered herself into the chair, she reached into her oversized handbag, fumbling around for something. When she didn't find what she was looking for, she began removing various items, piling them on my desk like it was a storage facility.

"Just a second," she said.

Several seconds later, she pulled out a plastic baggie containing a handful of photos, and she handed it to me.

I glanced inside the baggie. "What are these?"

"Pictures taken the night my best friend was murdered," she said. "Thought they might be useful."

"Useful how? I'm not sure why you asked to meet with me."

"Oh, isn't it obvious? I'd like to hire you to investigate a murder."

I nodded, opening my desk drawer and removing a notebook and a pen. "Why don't we start at the beginning?"

Zoey took a deep breath in. "A couple of weeks ago, Noelle threw an engagement party for me at her house. As the night wound down, and only a handful of us remained, we decided to have a toast. Noelle went upstairs to get more bottles of champagne, and not long after, the electricity—and all the lights and music—went out."

"For how long?"

"Five minutes, I guess. When all the lights came back on, Dominic screamed."

"Who's Dominic?"

"Noelle's husband. I ran upstairs to see what all the fuss was about and found him hovering over Noelle's body. At first, I thought she'd passed out. Dominic said she wasn't breathing, and I called 9-1-1. Not that it mattered. She was already dead."

"What was the cause of death?"

"She was strangled. And I … I just can't imagine why anyone would do something like that to her."

The tears came fast, and Zoey shoved a hand back inside her bag, pulling out a small package of tissues. She blotted her eyes, and I waited.

"I'm sorry," she said.

"You've just lost a close friend. It's understandable. Can I get you something to drink?"

"A glass of water would be nice. My throat feels like sandpaper."

I nodded and headed for the kitchen, grabbing her a glass of water and iced tea for myself. I returned to my office and handed her the glass, and she gulped half of the water down, using her hand to wipe the excess moisture off her face.

"This past month … it's been hard," she said.

"I bet."

"Four weeks ago, I was about to get married, and then a single moment changed everything."

"Did you postpone the wedding?"

"We did. I can't think straight, let alone go through with the wedding right now. Lucas, my fiancé, has been great, and so supportive. If I'm being honest, I think he's a bit relieved—about the wedding, not Noelle's death. The truth is, I was the one pushing to get married."

"Didn't Lucas want to get married?"

"Oh, yeah. It's just … he's been married before, and it didn't last long. The marriage was over in less than a year, but the trauma he went through left him with emotional scars. He'd vowed never to marry again."

"Why did he agree to give it another shot?"

"I've never been married before. It's always been a dream of mine, and he knows it. The day he proposed he said he never thought he'd ever be able to love anyone enough to walk down the aisle a second time until he met me." She looked at me, her eyes glossing over my left hand. "Are you married?"

"I was also married once before, and much like Lucas, I never planned to marry again either. Then I reunited with Giovanni, a man I went to college with, and … well, we admitted we've always had feelings for each other. We're getting married in August."

"What a great love story."

Indeed.

But she wasn't here to talk about weddings.

She was here to hire me to solve her friend's murder.

"Before the lights went out at your engagement party, how many guests were still at the house?" I asked.

She tapped a finger on the desk, thinking. "Let's see … including Noelle, Dominic, Lucas, and me, there were three other couples. Oh, and Kiera, Noelle's daughter."

"How old is her daughter?"

"She's five. Cutest little thing you ever did see. I can't imagine what she's going through."

"Where was Kiera when her mother died?"

"Upstairs, in bed."

"Did she see or hear anything?"

"She said she didn't."

"What about everyone else?" I asked. "Where were they?"

"Dominic had taken Kiera to bed about thirty minutes earlier, and he was still upstairs when Noelle was murdered. He said he was in the bathroom. The rest of us were downstairs."

"When the lights came back on, were all of the guests there with you?"

"Yes."

"What about your fiancé? Where was he?"

"He was outside, smoking a cigarette. He came inside as soon as Dominic screamed." She downed the rest of the water and cleared her throat. "Could I have some more water?"

I nodded and went to refill her glass.

Returning, I sat back down and said, "I'm assuming it was dark in the house when the lights went out."

"It was, we couldn't see a thing."

"What did everyone do when the lights went out?"

"We stood there, chatting, and wondering what to do."

"Did you hear anyone go up or down the stairs during the time the lights were out?"

She shook her head. "The stairs are made of solid wood. They're creaky and loud. I didn't hear anyone on them, but I suppose it's possible. I doubt it, though. Would have been hard to get up or down them in the dark."

Hard, not impossible.

"How's the investigation going so far?" I asked.

"I don't know. The first several days after the murder, Dominic was giving me updates. Then he stopped."

"Any idea why?"

"As the weeks have gone on, he's become more and more withdrawn. From what I understand, he's not talking much to anyone."

I handed her my notebook and pen. "Can you write down the names of all the guests who were there when Noelle died and their contact information, if you have it?"

"No problem."

She dug her phone out of her purse, using the directory to match phone numbers with names.

When she handed the notebook and pen back to me, I said, "Including those guests who'd left before the lights went out, how many people were at the party?"

"Around forty of our closest friends and family."

Forty.

A lot of people to interview.

The rest of them could wait.

I needed to focus on those who were there at the time of the murder first.

"Tell me about Noelle," I said. "Did she have a lot of friends? Was she well liked?"

"Noelle had tons of friends. She was such a good person, always doing things for others. She had a feisty side, though. It didn't come out much, but it was there."

"How feisty are we talking?"

"Hmm, might be best to give you an example. One time we were at a Brazilian steakhouse for lunch. It had been a while since the waiter had returned to the table, and I was after another glass of wine, so I got up to find him. I saw him at the front, chatting with the hostess. On my way over to him, I bumped into a woman, carrying a plate of food back to her table. The food flew off her plate, and it went everywhere. I turned to apologize to the woman, and before I could get any words out, she raised her voice, scolding me, using just about every expletive in the book."

"What did Noelle do?"

"She raced over, standing in front of me like a shield. She looked at the woman and said if she uttered another word to me, she'd take the exchange outside."

"*Outside* as in, she threatened to fight her?"

"Uhh, I mean, I feel like *threatened* is a bit harsh. She was being protective, that's all. When a person is in Noelle's inner circle, she has their back for life."

Maybe so, but a threat was a threat.

"What did the woman do after Noelle stood up for you?" I asked.

"She rolled her eyes, swished a hand in my direction, and walked off without saying another word."

"Sounds like Noelle shut her down."

Zoey let out a small laugh. "She sure did."

"Before she died, was there anyone she was feuding with … anyone you feel might have had a motive to kill her?"

"I don't know of anyone. Everything was going well in her life before she died. Her marriage was great, and they were talking about trying for another baby."

"Well, someone had it out for her."

"Someone did, which brings me to the reason I'd like to hire you. For one, I'd like to know what's going on in the police investigation. And for two … well, I've heard if the police can't find the person responsible for her murder, you can."

"I can, and I will."

Noelle's life was good.

Her marriage was good.

But something in her life wasn't.

And I was determined to find out what.

CHAPTER 3

Twisted Sister's "We're Not Gonna Take It" was blasting through the speakers when I entered the county coroner's office. It didn't take long for me to spot Silas, his hands in full air-guitar mode as he played along to the tune. Today he was dressed in his usual style—a Hawaiian shirt, linen slacks, and flip-flops. As the song's chorus bellowed in the background, he did a swift kick in the air and spun around, his eyes widening when he spotted me standing there, watching. Startled, he froze. Then he reached for a remote control and paused the music.

"I … ahh, hey, Georgiana," he said. "How long have you been standing there?"

"Long enough. Looks like you're having a fun day at work."

"Oh, I don't know about that. I'm on my lunch break, thought I'd blow off some steam."

Silas was one of the most laid-back, happy people I knew, making his comment about blowing off steam surprising.

"Is everything all right?" I asked.

"Wish I could say it was, but no, it's not. I kinda made a mess of things with Lana last night."

Silas and Lana had started dating several months before, and his relationship with her was one of the longest he'd ever had.

"What happened?" I asked.

"She broke up with me."

"Why?"

"She's pushing me to move in together."

Seemed a little soon to me.

"You two haven't been dating long," I said. "Four months, right?"

"Five, and I agree, it hasn't been long enough. Ask me, any talk about shacking up needs to wait until we hit the year mark."

"How did you respond when she suggested you two move in together?"

"I said I wasn't ready, and … well, it wasn't the response she wanted, that's for sure. She flipped out, started ranting about how she couldn't stay in a relationship with a person who didn't love her as much as she loved them."

How passive-aggressive of her.

"It's not true," he continued. "I've loved that woman from the moment I laid eyes on her. I just don't see the need to rush things, you know? If we're meant to be together, we will be. What's the rush?"

He leaned against his desk, crossed one leg in front of the other, and sighed, and I tried to muster up some words of encouragement.

"Maybe Lana just needs a little time to process the conversation you had last night," I said.

He shrugged. "Maybe. Doesn't feel good, though. Hasn't even been twenty-four hours since our little tiff, and I miss her like crazy."

"How did the conversation end?"

"She stormed out of my house, slammed the door, and drove off."

"Have you been in contact since then?"

He swished a hand through the air. "Nah, figured she needs some space to sort through her feelings. I'll be honest, I'm bummed out. I thought we had something special, something different than the ladies I've been with in the past."

Different was good.

We'd been friends for years, and while he'd dated here and there, he didn't commit to women often, which led me to believe he'd end up a lifelong bachelor. He'd always been a free spirit, a man who didn't like being tied to anything for too long ... well tied down to anything other than his surfboard.

"How is Lana different than the other women you've dated?" I asked.

"It's the connection we have—or *had,* I guess. Never felt anything like it. She's the best thing that's ever come into my life ... aside from you, I mean."

He offered me a cheeky grin, and we both laughed.

"Have you told Lana how you feel about her?" I asked.

"I've said things here and there, sure."

"Have you told her what you just told me?"

"No, guess I haven't."

"Why not?"

"I get a little tongue-tied talking to her about deep stuff. I get nervous around her—butterflies, you know? It's different, talking to you. We're buddies. We have history."

"We do. Lots of good memories over the years."

"With Lana, we're still in those early days of getting to know each other. I've been a little paranoid about messing up, and for good reason. I just did."

"Relationships aren't perfect. She should know that. If she wants to move in, it tells me she's trying to create a future with you, which isn't a bad thing, even if the timing isn't right."

He ran a hand along his forehead, pushing his bangs out of his eyes. "I need your advice, Gigi. Do you think I should ... you know, reach out to her in some way? Or should I wait?"

"How about doing a subtle check-in?"

"Not sure what you mean."

"Start off easy. Send her a text message. Keep it brief, let her know you're thinking of her. Tell her you hope she's doing all right, or you hope she's having a good day … something like that."

He wagged a finger at me, "Good idea. Should I do it now or …?"

"Now's good."

He reached into his pocket and pulled out his phone. "You don't mind?"

"Not at all."

I waited while he typed out his message one finger at a time, deleted it, typed it again, deleted it and then nodded, satisfied on his third try.

"And … sent," he said. "I'm all yours. Figure you're here for a reason. What's up?"

"Maybe my reason for stopping by is to check in and see how you've been."

"As much as I appreciate that, we check in every Friday at the coffee shop. You get a new case, or something?"

"I did. I've just been hired to investigate the death of Noelle Winters."

"Ahh, I wondered if you'd wind up getting involved. Her friend came here. Pushy little lass. She was asking all kinds of questions about the autopsy. I wanted to help her, but I, you know … I can't."

"When Zoey came to see me this morning, she said Noelle was strangled."

"Yep."

"Manual or ligature?"

"Manual."

"I'm sure you've heard the electricity at Noelle's house went out on the night she was murdered. It was out for five minutes or so. She was alive before the electricity went out, and dead when it came back on. Is five minutes enough time to strangle someone to death?"

"You betcha. When a person is being strangled, they lose consciousness within seconds. The pressure alone blocks the veins and arteries in the neck, stopping the flow of oxygenated blood to the brain."

"I knew it happened fast, but not that fast."

"A mere eleven pounds of pressure is all that's needed to cut off blood flow."

"Leaving the victim with permanent brain damage."

"You're right. Brain damage within thirty seconds, and death shortly thereafter."

In the past, I'd only had one case involving strangulation, and it taught me a lot. Based on statistics in strangulation cases over the years, women were strangled six times more often than men, and often because the assailant was experiencing intense emotion and rage. I'd always found murder by way of strangulation different than the other ways one could kill a person. The interaction was far more intimate. It wasn't always about the murder itself. It was about the need to exercise power and control over the victim's next breath.

"Strangulation is an awful way for anyone to go, even if death comes quicker sometimes," I said. "It's just as terrifying."

"Yep, I agree."

"Is there anything else I should know as I get going on this case?" I asked.

"Still early days. If something comes up, I'll give you a holler."

I nodded. "All right, see you on Friday."

"Hang on a second. There's one other thing I should mention. The murderer left fingerprint indentations on Noelle's neck. Based on the size, I'm leaning toward a man, not a woman. If I'm wrong, and a woman is responsible, her hands are larger than most."

I turned. "Thanks for the tip."

"Any time. And hey, while I have you here, you ought to take a look at a few of the autopsy photos, so you can see the fingerprints for yourself."

"I'd appreciate it."

He reached into the top drawer of his desk, pulling out a file folder, and then handing it to me. I spent the next several minutes going over the photos. Silas was right. The marks on Noelle's neck were significant in size.

"I was told the husband was upstairs when Noelle died, and their five-year-old daughter was in her room."

Silas bowed his head, huffing out a heavy sigh. "Always sad when a child loses a parent."

"It is. Have you met Noelle's husband?"

"I have. He was at the house, talking to the police when I showed up."

"How was he?"

"Frantic. Broken up. Seemed genuine, though I suppose that's not my expertise. It's yours."

One last thought crossed my mind.

"I'm guessing, given there were so many people in attendance at the engagement party, it must be difficult for you to sort out fingerprints," I said. "Bet they were everywhere."

"Difficult doesn't even begin to describe it. It's like finding a matching brick in a stack of similar bricks. Could take months to sort them all out, which brings me to an even better solution."

"What's that?"

"You could do us both a favor—find the killer and save me the trouble."

He was right.

Months to sort through the plethora of fingerprints he'd collected at the crime scene was far too long.

I needed answers, and I needed them now.

CHAPTER 4

I was sitting in Chief Foley's office, explaining to him and Detective Whitlock that I'd be investigating Noelle Winters murder.

After I finished talking, Foley perked up and said, "I had a feeling you'd wind up working this case."

"You did?"

"Noelle's pesky friend keeps dropping by, trying to get us to cough up information."

"Can you blame her?" I asked.

"Blame her? No, I can't say I do," Foley said. "But the woman's been a thorn in my side, a thorn I'm hoping you'll manage to keep out of my way."

"I'll do my best," I said.

"She cornered me at the gas station," Whitlock said. "Felt like I was being shaken down. I don't know what she does for a living, but if she's not a lawyer, she's missed her calling in life."

Whitlock laughed.

Foley did not.

"Zoey just wants answers, and though she's friends with

Noelle's husband Dominic, she told me he's not talking to anyone much anymore."

"Why would he?" Foley said. "The man's mourning his wife. A bit hard to do it in peace with that friend around. Ask me, there isn't a peaceful bone in the woman's body."

"I'm glad you're on the case," Whitlock said. "Between the three of us, I'm sure we'll be able to solve her murder and bring peace to Noelle's loved ones."

I'd always admired Whitlock's optimism. He'd come out of retirement to become a detective again. We'd collaborated on several cases over the past four years, and though he was in his early seventies, the fact I'd always considered myself an old soul made it easy for us to bond.

"What do you know about the murder so far?" I asked.

"We've been conducting interviews," Foley said. "A whole lotta them."

"Have you come across any useful information?"

"Not much. None of the guests seem to have a motive. Most of 'em either didn't know Noelle, or if they did, they didn't know her well."

"We've crossed them off the suspect list … *for now*," Whitlock added.

"Did any of the guests see or hear anything around the time of the murder?" I asked.

"One of the women we spoke to was standing by the stairs when the lights went out."

"Who?"

Foley leaned to the side, reaching for a folder on his desk. Opening it, he added, "Let's see now, guest's name was Lenore Whittaker."

"How does she know Zoey and Lucas?"

"Get this, she's Lucas' ex-girlfriend, if you can believe it. Said she remained friends with him after they broke up."

Friends was one thing.

Attending the engagement party of your ex was another.

"How long ago did their relationship end?" I asked.

"It's been a couple of years. She admitted they get together from time to time."

"Do you mean they see each other, or are you saying they've had sex post breakup?"

Foley's face went red.

Whitlock, who seemed amused by Foley's expression, cleared his throat, like he was trying not to laugh.

"Who knows what they're doing," Foley said. "Not my business."

"What else did Lenore say?"

"She claims when she met Zoey, they became fast friends. Such a different world we live in today, isn't it?"

A world with all manner of different dynamics.

"What else did Lenore say?" I asked.

"Like I said before, she was standing by the stairs when the power went out. She swears no one went up or down the stairs during that time. Even with the commotion it caused, she insisted she would have heard someone if they were on the stairs at the time."

"Was Lenore there alone, or with a date?"

"If she was with a date, she didn't mention it," Whitlock said. "This might sound strange, but when we spoke, I got the impression she was flirting with me."

"It doesn't sound strange to me. You're quite the charmer when you want to be."

"I say it's strange because she's half my age. When our conversation ended, she told me she hoped we could talk again, and then she placed a hand on my arm, looked me in the eye, and declared she was single."

"Interesting," I said. "Everyone was accounted for when the lights came back on. Zoey told me the remaining guests were all standing around in the living room … well, except for Lucas, who was outside smoking a cigarette."

"Front yard or back yard?"

"I don't know. I didn't ask. Are there multiple ways to get into the house?"

"Front door, back door, and then a sliding glass door off the master bedroom balcony, which wasn't locked when we got there."

"If the killer didn't use the stairs, he had to have been upstairs hiding out somewhere," I said.

"Waiting for an opportune moment to strike," Whitlock said.

I stood a moment, trying to re-create the scene in my mind. "So the killer strangles Noelle, then makes his escape. The lights come back on, Dominic discovers his wife, and he screams."

"Right," Foley said.

But how did the killer escape from the second floor unseen?

"Tell me about the layout of Noelle's bedroom," I said.

"If you're trying to figure out how the killer got away, there's a balcony off the side of Noelle's bedroom. Our best guess is he either went out that way or through a window. None of the windows in her room have screens, and they're big enough for someone to get in and out. Bit of a leap to get to the ground, though. I wouldn't risk it myself."

If the killer knew it was his only option, I assumed he would.

"During the party, were any of the guests allowed upstairs?" I asked.

"When we spoke to Zoey, she said everyone was told at the start that the celebration was to be contained to the main level. They didn't want anyone milling around when it was time for the child to go to bed."

"If the killer turns out to be one of the guests, I'm guessing he crept upstairs during the party and hid out. It's possible the other guests assumed that person had left when they hadn't."

"I thought the same thing, except Zoey said she walked each

guest to the door when they left to thank them for being there on her special night."

"Every time I think I'm onto something, it gets all kinds of holes poked into it."

"Tell me about it," Foley said. "That's how we feel."

"If guests were not allowed upstairs, it would have made the second floor a lot easier for Silas to dust for prints."

"It was, and we were hopeful about it, at first."

"And then?"

"Upstairs, there were prints belonging to Noelle, her husband, her daughter, Zoey, and Lucas. No one else."

"And since Silas found fingerprint marks on Noelle's neck, I'm assuming the killer wasn't wearing gloves—not when he killed her, anyway."

I crossed my arms, tapping a foot to the ground, thinking.

"I know that look," Foley said. "What's swirling around in that head of yours?"

"This murder seems so personal in nature—not only personal but premeditated."

"Sounds logical."

"Who else have you spoken to, aside from the guests who attended the party?"

"We've talked to Zoey and Lucas, of course. Talked to the husband a few times, and his sweet daughter."

"That was hard," Whitlock said. "Always is when it comes to kids."

"We've also spoken to the neighbors on her street," Foley said.

"Any chance one of them has a security camera?"

"The couple living across the street from Noelle's house has a security camera. It was on and recording the night of the murder. Problem is, during the time we believe Noelle died, the video doesn't show anyone coming or going from her house. All it picked up was a stray cat."

Whitlock raised a finger. "Which brings me to my theory. The back of Noelle's house butts up against a mountainside. I think the killer hiked up to the house, snuck inside, and then after the murder, he made his escape the same way."

"What I don't understand is, why kill Noelle during the party, when so many other people were around? It doesn't make any sense."

Unless … the killer could have been making a plan to murder Noelle, but hadn't decided when the murder would take place. Perhaps something had set him off that day, and he couldn't wait any longer.

Secrets had a way of doing that to a person.

Was Noelle keeping a secret, one she was getting ready to tell?

CHAPTER 5

I stopped by Dominic's home, hoping he was there so we could talk. I noted two sedans in the driveway—a Maserati and a much older sedan that had seen better days. Based on the upscale neighborhood, one of them didn't belong.

I rang the doorbell, and a woman with long, blond, bouffant hair and a big smile came to the door. She was dressed in a fitted red dress which was a bit too small, but it did a perfect job of accentuating her every curve.

She gave me a once-over, pointing at my black-and-cream, drop-waist dress as she said, "Vintage. I like it."

I considered returning the compliment, but given I didn't share the same fervor for her dress as she did mine, I did not.

"Can I help you?" she asked.

"I'm here to see Dominic."

"He's not in the best of moods. Does he know you're coming?"

"He will in a minute."

She stood a moment, saying nothing.

"Who are you, and how do you know Dominic?" I asked.

"Who are *you,* and how do *you* know him?"

"I'm Georgiana Germaine. I'm investigating his wife's murder."

She moved a hand to her hip. "Huh, I met the detective working on her case. He didn't mention he had a partner."

"I don't work for the police department. I'm a private investigator."

"Someone hired you?"

I nodded. "Zoey Morgan."

"Ahh, figures. Sounds like something she would do."

"You still haven't told me who *you* are," I said, "or what you're doing here, or why you came to the door instead of Dominic when it's his house."

"I'm Lenore, and he asked me to see who was at the door, so I did."

"Lenore Whittaker? Lucas is your ex-boyfriend, right?"

"Wow, you know your stuff, don't ya? I guess you would, given you're a private detective and all."

"I heard you were still friends with Lucas, but what are you doing here, at Dominic's house?"

"I … well, I was thinking about him today, wondering how he was holding up. I feel just awful about what happened to his wife, and I decided to bring him and the little one a casserole, something they can heat up for dinner tonight. I didn't make it, of course. It's store bought, but we can keep that little tidbit between us."

"I wasn't aware you and Dominic knew each other."

She pressed a hand to her chest. "Oh, we don't, not well. We met the night of the engagement party."

"You were standing by the stairs when the power went out."

"I was, and I'll tell you the same thing I told the cute older detective I talked to the other day—no one went up or down the stairs while the lights were out."

"I imagine everyone was talking during that time, trying to

figure out when the power would come back on again. Maybe try to find some candles …"

"They were."

"In all the chaos, how can you be sure someone didn't slip by you?"

She gritted her teeth. "I'm telling you, they didn't."

From down the hall, a male voice shouted, "Lenore, are you still here? Who's at the door?"

"I sure am," she said. "I'm having a little chat with a private detective. She wants to talk to you."

"Tell her I'm not up to having visitors today."

"I'm sorry for what you're going through," I shouted. "But if we don't talk now, I'll keep coming back until we do. I've been hired to investigate your wife's murder. I just have a few questions. It won't take long."

"Wait here," Lenore said. "Let me go talk to him."

She turned and started down the hall.

I followed.

A few seconds later, she glanced over her shoulder, unimpressed.

"I told you to wait at the door," she said.

"I know, I heard you."

"Are you always this pushy?"

"I wouldn't use the word *pushy*. *Determined* is a much better word. In cases like this one, time is everything, and I don't have a moment to waste."

She shrugged. "Guess I see your point. Don't know if he'll talk to you, though."

She spoke about Dominic as if she knew him a lot better than she claimed.

Her snug dress made a lot more sense to me now. Looking around as we headed toward Dominic, at the house, the furnishings, and the elaborate safe I saw when I passed by the sitting room, Dominic had money—and plenty of it.

He was a widower.

She was single, and, I suspected, looking to mingle.

The casserole she'd brought had gained her entry into the house.

Well played, for a little strumpet.

Strumpet.

Perhaps I was being too hard on her, too judgmental. I knew little of her, and yet I'd already labeled her.

We found Dominic in the kitchen. He had a robe wrapped around him that wasn't tied, exposing a white tank top and boxer shorts beneath. His thick, salt-and-pepper hair was disheveled, and he was hunched over a bowl of cereal. He didn't look up when I sat across from him at the table. He just kept on eating, pretending like I wasn't there.

"My name is—"

He raised a hand, stopping me. "I know who you are. Zoey left me a message this morning, her third so far today."

"She told me you haven't spoken to her much since Noelle died."

He glanced down, noticing his open robe, and he tightened it around himself. "Haven't spoken to most people. Zoey never stops talking, you know? She's one of those high-energy types. You can only be around them for so long before you need a break. I'm not saying she's a bad person. She's great. She was a good friend to Noelle."

"She did seem to be a bit on the impatient side when we met, and I want you to know I'm not here to add to your stress."

"Sure you are."

"I'm trying to figure out who killed your wife and why as soon as I can."

"Catching the bastard won't bring her back. She's lost to me now … lost to me forever." Tears pooled in his eyes, and he closed them, wiping the tears away. "I think about that night all the time. I dream about it even. How could I be so close and not know what was happening to her? I could have saved her, and I didn't."

"You weren't aware she was in danger. If you did, I have no doubt you would have done everything in your power to save her."

He looked up at me for the first time, staring into my eyes, while fighting back more tears. Then he slid off the chair and took his bowl to the sink.

"Is your daughter here?" I asked.

"She's with Noelle's mother for a few days. I want her here, with me … it's just, I'm not the father she needs right now. Feels like I'm falling apart, and I don't want her to see me like that."

"It's understandable. How's she doing?"

Lenore, who had been standing a few feet away, leaned in as if anxious to hear his response, something he seemed to pick up on.

"Hey Lenore, I appreciate the casserole and your offer to help out around here, but I think I'd like to speak to the detective alone."

She did not seem thrilled with the comment.

Her expression soured, and she looked away, clearing her throat as she said, "Uh, yeah, okay. I get it. You, uhh, you let me know if there's anything I can do."

CHAPTER 6

With Lenore out of the way, it gave me the opportunity to have a more intimate conversation with Dominic, one I hoped would provide me with a possible direction to go in. But first … I had a burning question, one that would persist until I asked it, so I did.

"Does Lenore stop by often, or was today the first time she came by?" I asked.

"She's checked in here and there."

"The two of you don't know each other well, do you?" I asked.

"Not at all. Why?"

I crossed my arms, thinking how to best phrase my next comment. "Given my line of work, it's easy for me to be suspicious of people's motives."

"You think she has a motive other than offering to help me out?"

I spread my arms and glanced around the room. "You have a nice place, expensive taste from what I can see, and you're a widower. Maybe Lenore is genuine in her offer to help, or maybe she's trying to get her foot in the door and start something between the two of you."

Voice shaking, he said, "If she thinks there will ever be something between us, she's mistaken. Noelle is the only woman I'll ever love. I will never, *ever* be with anyone else."

It was a bold statement, raising more questions.

"When did you and Noelle first meet?" I asked.

"She was my high school sweetheart."

"I know it's tough to talk about your wife so soon after her death. If you think you could find it in yourself to do it, even for a short time, I would appreciate it. Any information you can give me sooner than later ..."

"Isn't there a way you can conduct your investigation and leave me out of it? I've already spoken to the police, and I answered their questions. Can't you just talk to them?"

"I can, and I have, but having a separate conversation with you gives me a better picture of who your wife was and why someone murdered her." I paused, then added, "What if we don't discuss the night she died for now? What if we talk about her instead?"

After a long pause, he said, "I'll consider it. What do you want to know?"

"What was Noelle like in her day-to-day life? How did she spend her time? Did she have a lot of friends? Was she involved in the community in any way?"

Slow down, Georgiana.

Don't overwhelm the guy.

"You've hit me with a lot of questions," he said. "I'm not sure where to begin."

"Why don't we start at the beginning? How did the two of you meet?"

"I'd like to skip over that part of our lives for now, if you don't mind."

I wondered why, but I didn't press the issue.

"All right," I said. "How about you tell me whatever you feel comfortable sharing about her."

He took a deep breath in. "When my grandfather died, I inherited a large sum of money. I was young, in college at the time. Growing up, my grandfather had taught me a lot about how to make money with money, so I put a fair amount of what I'd inherited into the stock market and various other places."

I wasn't sure what his money habits had to do with Noelle, or where he was going with the conversation, but I kept quiet, hoping if he kept talking, it would all make sense.

"By the time I married Noelle, we were set for life," he continued. "I didn't even have to work, but I like working. It gives me purpose, so I became a partner and an investor in various start-ups I believed in. Noelle didn't come from money, and it meant a great deal to me to give her the life she deserved. We were happy here. So happy."

"Did Noelle work?"

"Not in a formal way. I wanted her to focus on herself, on her hopes and dreams. We both loved to travel, and we did a lot of it together, first by ourselves, and then with our daughter. Noelle also enjoyed her volunteer work. Giving back to the community meant a lot to her."

"Where did she volunteer?"

"A few different places, but most of her free time was spent at the women's center. It's a place for abused women looking for a fresh start in life."

"How long did she volunteer?"

"Up to her dying day. She felt the center was the one place she could contribute the most. She connected to the women on a personal level, and they trusted her."

He'd just told me a lot more than he realized.

He'd said the women connected to Noelle on a personal level.

They trusted her, which told me she empathized with their situations.

Empathy was different than sympathy.

Sympathy came from a place of feeling sorry for another's misfortune.

Empathy was rooted in understanding what the other person was going through, often because the person had experienced some version of the same thing themselves.

I needed to know more.

"Did something happen in Noelle's past that helped her bond with the women at the center?" I asked.

Dominic leaned back in the chair, crossing one leg over the other, going silent. If I were to coax an answer from him, I needed to try harder.

"I get the feeling you don't want to talk to me about some things in Noelle's past, and I understand," I said. "She was everything to you, and from listening to what you've said about her today, it's clear to me that protecting her, in the past and present, is a major priority to you."

"You're right. Protecting Noelle and Kiera means everything to me."

"I understand your hesitation in sharing private things with me," I said. "Whatever it is, if you trust me enough with it, I won't share it with anyone else unless I have to do so. You have my word."

He cleared his throat, once, then a second time. Then he began fidgeting, drumming his fingers on the table, sighing, shaking his head, no doubt thinking about what he wanted to say and what he didn't. Or maybe not saying anything at all.

"Before, when you asked how we met, I didn't want to talk about it because of the story behind it," he said. "How we came together … well, it's bittersweet. Even so, it was the start of us, a light in a very dark time. It led to us dating, and then getting married. But before all that, there was a heaviness hanging over both of us, an experience we endured together, one I wish wouldn't have happened the way it had."

I may not have understood everything he was trying to say, but one thing was clear. Noelle had endured something heavy and dark, and he had helped her through it, and kept her secret—if, in fact, she had one.

"Whatever happened in the past, you can tell me," I said.

"If she was still alive, I wouldn't tell you, or anyone. Now that she's passed away … well, I still wouldn't mention it to most people. Given you're investigating her murder, I suppose I feel all right about sharing it with you. Though I don't know how talking about it will help you with your case."

"Sometimes the smallest thing ends up meaning the most."

He nodded, exhaling a heavy breath. "In our sophomore year of high school, I was walking through the park one night, and I saw Noelle sitting inside her car. She was alone, and she was crying. We'd had a couple of classes together at school, but we didn't know each other well at the time. Still, the look on her face gave me cause for concern."

"What did you do?"

"I walked over and knocked on the driver's-side window. She looked up at me, and I noticed her bottom lip was bleeding. There was also a bruise on her cheek. I thought she might have been in an accident at first, but I didn't notice anything wrong with the car when I walked up. I asked her if she was okay."

"What did she say?"

"Nothing at first. She just stared at me, so I asked a second time. She told me she didn't want to talk about it, and she asked me to go away. Something inside me knew I needed to stay, so I did. I leaned against the car and stood there for a while, listening to her cry. Some time passed, and she seemed to calm down a little, so I started talking to her about anything that came to mind. I'd say it was a good hour before she relaxed enough to roll the window down."

"What happened then?" I asked.

"The first thing I noticed was the dress she was wearing. It was light blue with big, white polka dots. I'll never forget it. One of the sleeves was ripped, and it was then I thought someone may have assaulted her."

I crossed one leg over the other. "Did you ask her about it?"

"I did."

"What did she say?"

"She said she'd gotten into a fight with her boyfriend a few hours earlier, a kid we went to school with named Gabe Romero. He'd always had a temper on him, but I was still surprised he'd gotten angry enough to take it out on her. She admitted he'd gotten a little rough, and that's all she would say."

"Did you believe her?"

"Not one bit. Like I said before, we didn't know each other well, so I didn't feel right about pressing her to talk about it. She didn't seem in the right mental state to drive, so I offered to get her home, and she accepted. When we pulled into the driveway, and we both got out of the car, she ran over to me, pulled me close, and threw her arms around me. She turned to head into the house, and I reached out, grabbing her hand. I don't know why I did it. I just did. She turned back, and in that moment, all I wanted to do was to protect her. It was then I knew she was the woman for me."

Even though their relationship began in a horrible way, it still was a beautiful beginning to their love story.

"Did Noelle ever tell you more about what happened that night with Gabe?" I asked.

"Not right away, not until she felt safe enough to share it with me. Gabe didn't just rough her up because he was angry. He did it because that night he forced himself on her, pushing her to have sex. She did what she could to fend him off, inciting his anger. He hit her, and then he raped her."

He. Raped. Her.

Rape.

The word itself sent a shiver down my spine.

No wonder she'd spent her adult life trying to help others overcome their own misfortunes. In ways, I was sure it was therapeutic—a way for her to help herself, and others, to move on.

"It must have been hard for her to tell you what happened," I said.

"It took about four months before she told me. Before then, she told everyone she'd fallen down some stairs in the hallway after school. Some believed her, some didn't. When the truth came out, I'd like to think I was the one who convinced her to talk to the police."

"You were in the right place at the right time," I said.

"I've never seen it that way. If I'd been there before it happened, I could have stopped him, saving her from the nightmare that animal had put her through."

Dominic stood, rubbing a hand along his face.

"Are you all right?" I asked.

"Of course I'm not all right. I don't want to talk about this stuff anymore. It's too … it's too hard."

I was learning so much and wanted to continue. At the same time, I didn't want to pressure him into overload when he was hurting. I'd arrived at the house with so many questions about the fact he was mere feet away from his wife when she was murdered. I'd even considered him a suspect. Now, getting to know him, my conscience told me he was innocent, that everything he was telling me was true.

I was just about to suggest we get together another day when he looked at me and said, "Can we take a break?"

A break was far different than asking me to leave.

"Sure," I said. "Whatever you need."

"Five or ten minutes?"

"You got it."

He walked to the pantry, reaching up to the top shelf as he pulled out a bottle of rum. He gave me a nod and then exited the kitchen, bottle in hand, and I sat there, watching him turn the corner, tears streaming down his face as he disappeared down the hall.

CHAPTER 7

Several minutes later, I was beginning to think Dominic wasn't coming back to finish our conversation. I decided I'd wait another few minutes, then call out to him. If he didn't respond, I'd leave a note and show myself out.

Another few minutes passed, and to my surprise, I heard a door crack open. Dominic returned to the kitchen, still in his robe and looking even worse than before. He'd returned without the bottle of rum. I wondered where it was and how much he'd drunk, though I wasn't about to question him about it.

The man was grieving.

If a bottle of rum helped him get through the day, who was I to judge?

"Sorry for the wait," he said, sliding back into the chair. "I wanted to talk to my daughter, tell her I love her."

"I understand. You're a good father."

"I don't know about that, but thank you."

"Are you ready to continue our conversation?"

"I am. And hey, you can ask me anything, all right?"

Ask him anything?

What happened to the standoffish guy I'd met when I arrived, the one who wasn't interested in having a conversation?

Liquid courage, perhaps.

"When I first got here, you didn't want to talk," I said. "Now it seems you do, and while I appreciate it, I guess I'm questioning why you changed your mind?"

"Let's just say I had a change of heart."

A change of heart.

Even if he'd indulged in a fair amount of liquid courage, it worried me and didn't make sense. Something was off. I just couldn't put my finger on it.

"I want to keep going," I said. "I've learned so much about Noelle from our conversation today. But I also know the toll it must be taking on you."

He waved a dismissive hand. "Don't worry about me. All I ask is one thing—get all your questions out, right here, right now. Deal?"

"Deal."

I'd been mulling a few over during our break.

"What happened after Noelle told the police about Gabe?" I asked.

"He was arrested and convicted of the crimes he'd committed against her. I should also tell you that during the trial another teen came forward, a girl he'd dated the year before. He'd assaulted her once, slapped her across the face, but she wasn't raped."

"Did the girl say what happened?"

"Same reason. He was pressuring her for sex."

And yet, he hadn't forced himself on her the way he had with Noelle, which told me his violent temper had escalated from one woman to the next.

"What sentence did Gabe receive at trial?" I asked.

Dominic yawned, covering his mouth as he said, "He was supposed to be locked up for eight years, but he was out in six—

good behavior and all that bull crap. No idea what happened to him after he was released. Haven't seen him since he got out."

"Did Gabe ever try to contact Noelle?"

"Not in person. He wrote her a letter while he was in prison, though. It was full of apologies, telling her he still loved her, and he was committed to getting the therapy he needed so he wouldn't ever do what he did to her to another woman again. I thought it was nonsense, that he'd sent the letter to make himself look apologetic so he could convince everyone he'd changed. Guys like Gabe, they don't change."

"What did he have to say for himself at the trial?"

"I expected him to come in all full of himself, denying what he'd done. He surprised me when he did the opposite. He admitted it, all of it, and said he regretted the assault and the rape. He acted like he didn't know what came over him, like he'd been possessed or something."

"Was he going for an insanity plea?"

"You'd think so, but he said he wanted to be locked up for what he'd done. He also said being behind bars would give him the opportunity to change his ways and not hurt anyone else."

I wasn't sure what to make of it.

Was it a ploy to get a reduced sentence?

If so, it had worked.

I wondered where Gabe was now, and what he'd done with his life after getting out of prison. I made a mental note to find him and see what he was up to nowadays. And I wanted to verify he had no involvement in Noelle's murder.

"I appreciate you sharing Noelle's story with me," I said. "Do the police know about it?"

"I thought about telling them—" he shrugged, "—but in a way, it felt like I'd be betraying her if I did. Feels like I'm betraying her now, telling you."

"If it helps me to find out who killed her and why, it will all be worth it."

"Yeah, well … I'm assuming we're done, with that subject, anyway. What other questions do you have?"

I considered what I hadn't asked yet.

"Was there anyone in Noelle's recent life who had a problem with her, anyone who would have wanted to harm her?" I asked.

"I've thought a lot about that in the past week. The police asked me the same thing. Truth is, I can't think of a single person, or even why anyone would do what they did to her. I mean, sure, there's what happened in the past, and I considered Gabe might be involved. Thought about finding him, but right now, it wouldn't be a good idea. My head's not on straight. If I thought he did it, I don't know if I could control myself …"

"Leave Gabe to me. I'll find him, and I'll talk to him. If he had anything to do with her death, he'll pay for what he's done."

"I'm holding you to it."

I thought back to what he'd said about Noelle's time at the women's center. "I was wondering … did Noelle ever share the story about what happened to her with any of the women at the center?"

Dominic let out a long sigh. "From time to time, but I don't know who she told and who she didn't. It wasn't something she liked talking about. Every time she did, it took a toll on her."

I nodded, waited for him to continue.

"I believe it was because she never moved past it, not all the way. Talking about it triggered her, and she knew it. But if she felt she could reach a woman who wouldn't have otherwise spoken out about what she was going through, Noelle used her story to give them the confidence they needed to let it all out."

"What happened when a woman came to the center and confessed their abusive experiences?"

"If Noelle thought there was a chance she could convince them to contact the police, she'd try her best to talk them through it."

I wondered how many cases the police had been involved in,

how many men received jail time, or worse, and how many knew of Noelle's direct involvement.

"Did you ever worry that Noelle's work at the center could blow back on her in some way?" I asked.

He folded his arms, leaning back in the chair. "I'll tell you something I didn't tell you before, something most people don't know. Noelle didn't just volunteer at the center. She founded it. I offered to open the center because I knew how much it meant to her, but my support came with a few rules."

"What were your rules?"

"For starters, she had to use a different name. The center was named the Ophelia Albrecht Women's Center. Ophelia was Noelle's grandmother's name, and Albrecht was my grandmother's maiden name."

"Are you saying the women who came to the center thought your wife's name was Ophelia Albrecht?"

"That's what I am saying, yes."

Clever.

"What about when the women went to the police?" I asked. "I imagine Noelle sat in on some of those conversations. I'm sure some of the women would have wanted her there for support."

"You're right—she did go to some of those police meetings. They knew about the alias. They understood why it was necessary, and they praised us for it."

If Noelle had been working with the police at the San Luis Obispo Police Department, Foley and Whitlock would have worked with her, which meant they would have known about Noelle's background when they discovered she'd been murdered. Yet neither of them had said anything to me, making me believe that even though she lived in the county, it was possible the women's center was outside of it.

"Where is the center located?" I asked

"Santa Maria."

Santa Maria was about an hour's drive from Cambria, and

just as I'd suspected, it was in a different county, Santa Barbara County.

"Why set up the center in Santa Maria and not closer to home?" I asked. "An hour's drive isn't bad, but it's still a bit of one."

"Santa Maria is where we got engaged."

"I see. The city had a special meaning to you both."

"It also has a population of over four hundred thousand people. Half of those people are women."

An interesting point, though I felt I'd taken the conversation about Noelle and the center as far as I could—for now.

"What other hobbies or things was your wife involved in?" I asked.

"Tennis. She loved it, played since she was fourteen." He paused, then added, "I want to show you something."

He excused himself, and I watched him walk to the living room, grabbing a gold frame off the mantel. He brought it back and handed it to me.

The photo was of a younger woman, around eighteen, I guessed. There was no mistaking the woman was Noelle. In her hands was a trophy. From the looks of it, she'd won first place, but that wasn't all I noticed. Though she was smiling, there was something haunting in her eyes. Perhaps the aftermath of the trauma she'd been through with Gabe. In the background, I noticed a younger version of Dominic, smiling and staring at Noelle like he was so proud, her biggest supporter.

If what he had said about their relationship was true, I couldn't imagine the hurt he was experiencing now or how hard it would be for him to get through such a loss.

"Did Noelle play tennis throughout her adult life?" I asked.

"She did, except for the first several months after our daughter was born."

I handed the picture back to him, and he stared at it for a time, rubbing a thumb over Noelle's face. Then he raised the frame over his head and did something unexpected. He hurled it across the room, the glass shattering as it hit the wall, spitting shards all over the wood floor.

The tears returned, and he leaned over the counter, bowing his head.

"I'm so sorry, Dominic," I said. "Maybe you need to get some rest. If this is too much, I understand. I know you wanted to get all of this out in one visit, but I don't feel like you're up to continuing right now."

"It's just … she was my entire life. Don't get me wrong, I love our daughter, but our daughter is a part of her. I can't look at her without seeing Noelle. She's her spitting image and has been ever since the day she was born."

"It might be too much to process right now, but time has a way of helping you heal. I'm not saying the pain will ever be gone. It won't. I'm saying pain goes through phases."

"What would you know about losing the love of your life?"

"Nothing, but I know a hell of a lot about losing a father way too soon—and a daughter."

"You lost a daughter?"

"I did."

"How old?"

I paused, then, "She didn't live long enough to start kindergarten."

"How do you deal with it?"

"I take it one day at a time, and I try to focus on the positive things in my life, just like you can focus on the positive things in yours—including your daughter."

He was sobbing now.

"It's not the same!" he shouted. "And I'm not you! I can't just push it down, pretend everything is going to be okay."

I didn't push it down.

And I never pretended everything was okay.

Still, I remained silent.

If he needed to lash out at someone, he could lash out at me.

I remained silent because I wanted him to feel in control of the narrative. But as the moments ticked by, it seemed he was slipping further away from me and into his own suffering. The tears poured out of him now, like a hazy sky bursting open with a downpour of torrential rain.

He wiped his eyes with a hand and said, "Forgive me. I shouldn't have spoken to you the way I did just now. I know you're trying to help."

"There's nothing to forgive, Dominic."

"I thought I could, but I can't. I can't do this anymore. Excuse me."

He turned and took off down the hall. I thought he was going for more rum at first, but then, from down the hall, I heard eleven of the worst words I'd ever hear, "Tell my daughter I love her, and tell her, I'm sorry."

I shot up, running down the hall toward him.

But I was too late.

I heard a distinct click, a familiar click.

And then … *boom.*

CHAPTER 8

I fell to my knees, my body trembling as I reached up to open the bedroom door, knowing what I'd find inside, and I was right. Dominic was on the ground, blood pooling around him. He'd shot himself in the head, and from the looks of it, the single shot had done what he'd intended. I reached my shaky hand toward his neck, feeling for a pulse, knowing there wasn't one.

A minute earlier, he was sitting next to me, talking.

Now, he was dead, and I was forced to make a call I didn't want to make.

I made it anyway.

As every fiber of my being shot spasms throughout my body, I crawled over to the wall, leaning my head against it. It felt like I was there for hours … then, I felt a hand on my shoulder and a familiar voice, calling out to me through the fog encapsulating my brain.

"Georgiana, it's me," Whitlock said. "Everything's going to be okay. I'm here. Foley's here. And I want you to know I've called Giovanni and told him what happened. He's on his way. Should be here soon."

"I … thank you."

I wanted to say more, but in this moment, they were the only three words I managed to get out.

"What can I do for you?" he asked. "Would you like some water or …?"

"You can get me out of here, out of this room."

His arms circled around me, pulling my ragdoll body to a standing position. He guided me to the door and then down the hall to the sofa. He lowered me down, and I pushed myself into a sitting position, pulling my knees up and wrapping my arms around them as I buried my head, hiding my tears.

"Foley's waving me over," Whitlock said. "I'll be right back, okay?"

"Yeah, sure, okay."

He left my side, and I heard whispers from across the room—Whitlock and Foley talking. I thought Foley would come over, console me, ask questions … *something*, but he didn't. Perhaps he thought it best to give me the time I needed to process what had happened first.

I heard the front door open, and I wiped my eyes, glancing up to see who'd just come in. Silas entered the living room and looked around, making a beeline for me as soon as we made eye contact.

"Hey, Gigi," he said.

"Hey."

"How you holding up?"

"I'm not."

"I heard what happened, and I'm sorry."

"Yeah, me too."

He sat beside me, draping an arm around my shoulders. "I know it doesn't seem like it right now, but you're going to be okay. You're the strongest woman I know."

I let out a frustrated grunt, pounding a fist into the sofa. "I know I will be all right, but it shouldn't have happened, not on my watch. I should have known he was about to take his life. The longer Dominic and I had talked, the more I could tell something was off. There were clues, signs I picked up on, but not enough to put it all together. If I had, I could have saved him."

"Even if what you're saying is true, you couldn't have been here for him day and night. If he'd decided to end his life, it would have happened one way or another."

"He has a daughter. I know he felt lost without his wife, but how could he do what he did—rob her of a father so soon after she lost her mother?"

"I don't know."

I took a deep breath in. "I'm so angry … at myself, at him."

"You have a right to feel that way."

"We had a good talk, before he … you know, killed himself. I can't help but wonder if something I said drove him over the edge."

"Come on, Gigi. You're beating yourself up over a decision *he* made … not you, *him*."

"Maybe you're right. I just … I haven't had something like this happen in a long time."

"We never know what we're going to face in the line of work we're in."

He was right.

Our jobs came with risks, and today, I'd been reminded of just how harsh those risks could be.

"Dominic shot himself in his room," I said. "I'm guessing it's where everyone is right now."

"I can stay with you for a few more minutes."

"Best to look at him as soon as you can."

"I don't want to leave you."

"I appreciate it. You're a good friend, but you have a job to do. We can talk again later."

Silas turned, and I saw Giovanni standing over him. He placed a hand on Silas' shoulder and said, "Go and do what you came here to do. I've got her."

Silas nodded, offering me a smile as he headed down the hall.

Giovanni took one look at me, extended his hand, and said, "Let's get you out of here, love."

"I don't want to leave," I said. "I need to stay. I need to tell everyone about my visit with Dominic. They need to know what happened."

"There will be plenty of time for all that later. I'll speak to Whitlock and Foley and let them know they're welcome to come by the house when they're done here, *if* you're up to talking to them."

The thought of leaving didn't feel good.

It felt awful, almost like a betrayal, though I didn't know why.

I didn't pull the trigger, I didn't end his life, so why did I feel like I did?

CHAPTER 9

A few hours later, Foley and Whitlock came by the house. Giovanni met them at the door. They chatted for a time and then were escorted to the den, where they found me dressed in silk pajamas and fuzzy slippers, sipping a cup of tea.

They both took a seat, saying nothing at first, as they offered awkward smiles in my direction like I was a delicate damsel in distress.

"How are you doing, kiddo?" Foley asked.

Kiddo.

To Foley, the word was a term of endearment.

To me, it was a bit hysterical, given I was five years his senior, but I appreciated the sentiment, nonetheless.

"I'm a bit numb, I guess," I said. "The more I go over my visit with Dominic, the more upset I am with myself. I keep thinking I could have prevented him from killing himself somehow."

"Dominic made his own choice," Foley said. "You may have been there when it happened, which was unfortunate, but it was still his decision."

"Then why do I feel so guilty?"

"Because you have a heart."

"I may have pushed him too hard, overwhelmed him during our conversation."

"You didn't hold the gun to his head. He made that decision all on his own."

"If it makes you feel any better, we found a letter on the nightstand in his bedroom," Whitlock said. "It was addressed to his daughter. He planned to take his own life today, and whether you were there or not, I'm inclined to believe it wouldn't have made a difference. His mind was made up."

"I couldn't agree more," Foley said. "The fact you were there may have put it off for a couple of hours, but even if you figured out what he was planning, I doubt you could have stopped him."

Hearing this information should have made me feel better.

It didn't.

"What did the letter say?" I asked.

"It was short," Foley said. "He wanted his daughter to know he loved her. He said not to be sad because he was in heaven, taking care of her mother. And then he mentioned something about the two of them watching over her for the rest of her life."

I huffed an irritated, "Is that supposed to make her feel better about what he did?"

In this instance, it seemed like a selfish act, plain and simple.

She was grieving the death of her mother, and he doubled down on that grief by committing suicide.

Foley and Whitlock exchanged worrisome glances.

"What is it?" I asked.

"You're … uhh, well, angry, which is understandable," Foley said. "You've had one heck of a day. If you want to wait to talk about your visit with Dominic, we can, but maybe we should regroup tomorrow, talk about it then."

Foley went quiet, waiting for my response.

He was right.

I was heated.

The tension inside me was rising like magma about to erupt.

I finished the last of my tea, setting the cup on the side table.

While I stewed on my thoughts, Giovanni entered the room, addressing the men as he said, "Can I offer you both a drink?"

"I'd love one, but I'm still on the clock," Foley said.

Whitlock laughed. "After what we've been through today, I say we toss the clock out the window."

"Great idea," Giovanni said. "What can I get for you?"

"Bourbon on the rocks, if it's not too much trouble."

Giovanni nodded and turned toward Foley. "And you?"

Foley huffed a long sigh, as if wrestling with his decision. "I'll have the same, I guess. Why not?"

Giovanni scooped up my empty mug and left the room, returning a minute later with three bourbons and a glass of sparkling wine. He handed the glass of bubbles to me, planting a kiss on my forehead as he said, "A bit of bubbly might do your stomach some good."

It would also take some of the edge off.

We raised our glasses, and Giovanni said, "Here's to solving this murder."

Foley took a sip of bourbon and winced.

Lightweight.

"Toward the end of my visit with Dominic, he talked about Noelle's love of tennis," I said. "He even got up to get a picture so I could see her in her younger years. In the photo, she was holding a trophy she'd won at one of her matches. I thought he was doing all right, and then, he stared at the photo, and he lost it."

"Lost it, how?"

"He started crying uncontrollably. I tried to offer him a few words of comfort, saying things like I understood what he was going through. It seemed to work for a moment, and then it backfired, and he bolted out of the room for a second time during our conversation. Seconds later, he spoke to me from down the hall. They were the last words he said before he committed suicide."

"What did he say?"

"He said to let his daughter know he loved her, and he said he was sorry. In that moment, I knew what he was about to do, and I tried to save him. I raced toward his room. It was seconds before I got to him, but I was still too late. When I entered the room, he'd already sagged to the ground, the gun on the floor next to him, and he was lying in a pool of his own blood."

Giovanni set his bourbon down and sat next to me, wrapping an arm around me as he said, "I'm so sorry, *cara mia*."

"We're sorry, too," Whitlock said. "Doesn't matter how many times something like that happens in our presence, it's still one of the worst things a person can witness."

"I still can't help but wonder if something I said or he did had led to him pulling the trigger." I rubbed my forehead. "But knowing he left a letter … I guess it changes things. He planned to kill himself, and there was nothing I could have done to save him."

CHAPTER 10

I indulged in a bit more of the bubbly, and I thought about how much there still was to discuss about my visit with Dominic. I was tired, my head throbbing, but what I had to say couldn't wait until tomorrow.

"I appreciate your offer to discuss Dominic later, but since the two of you are here now, I say we keep talking and make the most of this horrible day," I said.

"You sure?" Foley asked.

"I am. We need to catch Noelle's killer. He, or *she*, may have only committed one murder, but in my mind, I'm holding that person responsible for two. Dominic would still be alive if Noelle wasn't murdered."

"How can you be so sure?" Foley asked. "Maybe the guy wasn't happy, even before the murder."

"I don't think so. I think he lived and breathed for his wife, and I feel they had a deep love for each other."

"What did you learn during your conversation with him?"

"I learned I'd been going about it all wrong."

"How so?"

"I started at the end with you guys, but I should have started at the beginning. I first arrived at Dominic's house with the intent to learn more about Noelle and what she was like when she was alive. I knocked on the door, expecting Dominic to answer it, but he didn't. Lenore Whittaker did."

"Lenore Whittaker? Isn't she the woman who used to date Lucas Bronson, the guy who's marrying your client?" Foley asked.

"Yep."

"She doesn't even know the guy, does she?"

"Not well. They met at Lucas and Zoey's engagement party."

"I don't understand."

"I didn't either, and I questioned her about it. She said she'd been thinking of him today, so she decided to bring him a casserole. Here's the interesting thing. Today wasn't the first time she'd stopped in to see him. She's been there a few times, and maybe even more than a few times."

"Huh, strange. What do you make of it?"

"I think Lenore's a gold digger. She saw an opportunity, and she jumped on it. I could be wrong, but I bet I'm right. Dominic didn't seem interested in talking to me at first, but after he asked Lenore to leave, he was a lot more forthcoming. I'm guessing it's because he knew he was about to commit suicide—he decided he wanted to offer his help in my investigation while he could."

"What makes you so sure?"

"There were a few things I picked up on during our conversation. One minute, he didn't want to open up to me; the next, he did a complete one-eighty, telling me I could ask him anything. He said it was because he didn't want to talk about it again. But if he was getting ready to off himself, he relaized there wouldn't be a next time for us to talk again."

"I'm interested to hear what he had to say."

"He said a lot more than I thought he would. Right in the middle of our conversation, though, he grabbed a bottle of rum and excused himself to call his daughter. When he returned, he didn't seem to be doing well, but he still wanted to continue the conversation, so we did."

"The man wasn't doing well because he knew the conversation with his daughter was his last," Foley said.

Giovanni grabbed the bottle of bourbon off a nearby table, walked over to Foley and Whitlock, and served another round.

Foley, who'd been hesitant to drink just minutes before, took a hearty swig and said, "What topics did you two talk about?"

"Everything revolved around his wife. He told me about the night they first met, and about what she was like as a person. On that subject, there's something you should know, something Dominic told me in confidence."

Whitlock leaned in, intrigued. "Lay it on us."

"Noelle was assaulted and raped by a boyfriend when she was in high school."

Foley raised a brow. "Where's this boyfriend now?"

"His name is Gabe Romero. Dominic talked Noelle into turning Gabe in for what he'd done. At trial, Gabe pled guilty and was locked up for several years. He wrote Noelle a letter while he was in prison, but Dominic said they haven't seen or heard from him since he was released."

Whitlock reached into his pocket, pulling out a notebook and a pen. He flipped it open to a blank page and began writing.

"Get this," I said. "After Noelle was raped, she was sitting in her car at the park, and Dominic walked by. She was crying, and when he walked over, he noticed she had a bruise on her face and the sleeve of her dress was ripped. He didn't want to leave her, so he just stood there, talking with her, until she calmed down. That's how their relationship began."

Foley ran a hand along his forehead, his head shaking back and forth as he said, "That's one hell of a story."

"I know it sounds strange, but it was the beginning of their love story. He told me when they parted that night, he knew they were meant to be together. In the weeks that followed, they began dating, and after they graduated, they got married."

Whitlock crossed one leg over the other, wiggling the pen in his hand. "What a fascinating story. He never mentioned any of it to us. I'm not surprised he told you, but why do you think he did?"

It was the perfect question, a segue into what I was about to say next.

"Are either of you aware that Dominic and Noelle had opened a women's center?" I asked. "She was quite involved."

"No, we know nothing about it. I'm sure we would have found out sooner or later, but no one has mentioned it to us."

"After Noelle went through what she did with Gabe, she wanted to help other women who'd endured similar experiences, so they founded the center."

Foley looked at Whitlock. "I can't believe this is the first we're hearing about it."

"Me either," Whitlock said. "What more can you tell us about it, Georgiana?"

"Knowing these women were coming to the center to get away from their abusive situations, Dominic had some rules to keep Noelle safe."

"Rules like …"

"Not using her real name. The center is named the Ophelia Albrecht Women's Center. Ophelia was Noelle's grandmother's name, and Albrecht was Dominic's grandmother's maiden name. Noelle used that name when she spent time with the women there."

"Why was her husband worried about her using her actual name?" Foley asked.

"In some situations, Noelle convinced the women to talk to the police, see if there was any legal recourse for the abuse. I'm guessing some of these guys went to jail or prison for what they'd done, and I'm sure those men weren't too happy about that."

"Do you think someone found out Noelle's true identity, perhaps a disgruntled husband or boyfriend?"

"I think it's a strong possibility. I won't know until I poke around the place, talk to the people who work there."

"Where's the center located? It couldn't be around here, or I'd know about it."

"It's in Santa Maria," I said. "Dominic also mentioned that the officers over there were aware of Noelle's alias—and the reason why it was necessary."

Foley took another swig of bourbon, making the same face he'd made before. "Donnelly's the chief of police in that area. Met him a few times. Great guy. Guess the two of us need to have a little chat."

"If Noelle's killer was affiliated with the women's center in some way, I think we want to focus on any women who have made recent complaints."

"Good idea. I'll ask him. Anything else we should know before we get out of your hair?"

"Not that I can think of right now."

"All right, well then, it's getting late. We'll leave you, touch base tomorrow sometime. Get some rest now and try your best to shut off that mind of yours."

I smiled and nodded, knowing shutting off my mind after the day I'd had wouldn't just be hard, it would be near impossible.

CHAPTER 11

I woke not knowing how much sleep I'd gotten the night before. I knew it wasn't much, and given the numerous times I'd woken, I wasn't surprised that I was feeling a bit groggy.

Groggy or not, the mouthwatering aroma of bacon was enough to rouse me for the day. I sat up, turning toward Luka, my Samoyed, who was eyeing me with a look of concern. Given the smell of bacon was wafting through the house, I was surprised he'd remained by my side.

He laid his head on top of my lap, and I reached out, stroking his fur as I said, "I'm okay, bud. It was just a bad night of sleep."

He looked up at me, unconvinced.

Giovanni entered the room, whistling a classic jazz tune as he offered me a freshly brewed mocha.

"Your timing is perfect," he said. "Breakfast will be ready in about twenty minutes."

"Smells like bacon is on the menu."

"Yes, it's in the Mediterranean quiche that's baking."

Just what I needed to get the day going.

I took a sip of the mocha he'd given me and then set the mug on the nightstand. "I hope I wasn't too much of a pain to sleep next to last night."

"You tossed and turned throughout the night."

"Sorry."

"You don't need to apologize. Yesterday was a hard one, and you handled it with grace. How are you feeling today?"

Like I'd been flattened by a semitruck.

"I'm tired, and my head hurts," I said. "I'll survive."

"I can get you some ibuprofen."

He turned, and I reached out, grabbing his hand. "Hey, I know we were supposed to talk about our wedding plans this week."

"Don't trouble yourself with it now. We have time."

I wasn't so sure.

Time had a way of creeping up on a person until there was no time left.

We were set to be married in five months, and while we were making good progress, there was much to be done.

Our original plan was to have the wedding and reception in New York City, in the backyard at Giovanni's family's estate. It was a massive yard with beautiful gardens, the perfect place. Giovanni's sister, Daniela, my former college roommate, had been helping us with the arrangements.

"Five months will go by fast," I said.

"I'm sure it will. For now, we don't need to concern ourselves with every detail, not when you have a case to solve."

He shot me a wink and tapped a hand to his leg. Luka jumped off the bed, trotting alongside him as they disappeared down the hallway.

My thoughts turned toward our wedding. Everything was well in hand and organized, coming together without any major issues. Still, given I was an overthinker, it weighed on my mind. One thing I wouldn't be overthinking was the honeymoon. Giovanni was planning it as a surprise, and I couldn't wait to see what adventure he had in store for us.

I finished the mocha, showered, dressed, and joined Giovanni at the kitchen table. As I took a seat, I noticed he'd placed two tablets of ibuprofen on a napkin beside my plate, ever the gentleman. I scooped them up and popped them into my mouth, washing them down with a sip of orange juice.

"What's on your agenda for today?" he asked.

"After breakfast, I'll head to the office to meet with Simone and Hunter. I need to bring them up to speed on the case and let them know how they can help me with it. Then I'll get in touch with my client, Zoey Morgan. She called me four times yesterday."

Both Simone and Hunter were former detectives. Simone was also married to my brother, Paul. A few years earlier, when I'd started the agency, both ladies came to work for me.

"Did you take any of Zoey's calls?" he asked.

"Just the first one. She said nothing of importance, so I asked her to give me some time to interview a few people before I got back to her."

"How did that go over?"

"It didn't. She called an hour later. It irritated me, so I sent the call to voicemail, and the next call, and the next. We're going to need to set some boundaries. If I wanted to be micromanaged, I'd ask my mom to do a ride-along."

I laughed, and he said, "I have no doubt your mother would jump at the opportunity."

"She would. Don't get me wrong. I'm glad I took this case. I just hope I don't off the woman before I find out who murdered her friend."

We chitchatted through the rest of breakfast, and then I glanced at the calendar, noticing today's date. "I almost forgot you were flying to New York today for your monthly family meeting."

"About that … given what happened yesterday, I was thinking I'd sit this one out."

"I'm fine. You should go."

"Are you sure?"

"I am. How long will you be away?"

"Two, three days at most. My cousin Angelo wants to pitch an idea for a new hotel. There's a restaurant in a prime location in the heart of the city that may be closing its doors."

"A hotel? I'm intrigued. Has he offered any details about it?"

"According to Daniela, he's suggesting buying it and doing a complete remodel. I've seen photos of the existing hotel. The one thing we all agree on is it needs a lot of work before it becomes his idea of New York's next biggest hot spot."

"Does Angelo have a theme in mind?"

"Five-star art deco."

I smiled, and he added, "Given the '20s and '30s are your favorite era, I thought you'd be pleased."

I was, and my mind was racing with ideas.

"I love it," I said. "If you all sign off on it, I'd like to make a suggestion."

He leaned in. "What's the suggestion?"

"I'd add a classy, hidden speakeasy, requiring a password to gain entry. In terms of décor, I'd fill the place with mobster memorabilia, similar to what they have on display at the museum in Las Vegas."

"And where do you plan on getting this 'mobster memorabilia'?"

"We could start by looking in the attic at your family estate. I'm sure we'd find plenty of things in there."

I'd said it as a joke but knowing there was some truth to it.

"A speakeasy … not a bad idea," he said.

"As far as what happened in the past, your family's business dealings are legitimate now," I said. "Why not let the past and the present collide and give the customers a bit of history while they're sipping away on a mint julep?"

"It sounds interesting. I'm just not sure about the timing. I've given some thought to expanding my restaurant, opening a second location."

"Why not open it inside the hotel?"

"Another good idea. I'll see what Angelo has to say. He hired an architect to draw up his vision for the place. I'll look it over when I see him."

"Sounds like he's put a lot of thought into this dream of his."

"I agree."

Giovanni grabbed the napkin from his lap, wiping his mouth. Then he stood, reaching for his plate and mine. "Did you get enough to eat, amor?"

"I did."

"Good, if you need me for any reason while I'm away, you will call, won't you?"

I nodded, and my phone rang. Looking at the name on the caller ID, I saw it was Simone. I answered with, "I'll be heading to the office in about fifteen minutes."

"Good," she whispered.

"Why are you whispering?"

"Your client is here, and if she doesn't simmer down, I'm going to drop-kick her booty right on out the front door."

"Understood. Hang tight. I'll be there soon."

CHAPTER 12

I hadn't made it more than three steps inside the office before Zoey charged at me, her voice raised, demanding information about Dominic.

I squared off with her, lifting a finger as I uttered, "No."

"No … *what*?"

"If you want to have a conversation with me, you need to calm down and behave in a more civilized manner."

"I *am* being civilized. It's obvious you don't care about my feelings, or about what I'm going through!"

"Take a breath, Zoey, and then we'll have a conversation. Or don't, and we won't. It's up to you."

"You can't talk to me this way. I'm your client."

"Does being my client give you free rein to treat me any way you like? If you believe it does, you're mistaken."

Zoey fisted her hands, and I stepped back. For a moment, I thought she might attempt to strike me, but she didn't. She burst into tears and plopped down on the sofa, bawling into her hands.

I thought about consoling her in some way but decided against it. Perhaps the best thing to do was to give her a moment to work through her feelings.

I walked past her toward Simone and Hunter. I suggested they take a break and leave the office, returning for our scheduled meeting in an hour—a suggestion they were happy to accept. As they made their exit, I went to the kitchen, fixing myself a cup of tea, which I took to my office. Thinking some relaxing music might help ease the tension, I flipped through my playlists, finding one of my meditation soundtracks.

A few minutes went by and then Zoey stood, straightening her shirt before sauntering in my direction.

She entered the office and crossed her arms, looking at me like she was waiting for me to say something.

"Are you feeling any better?" I asked.

"I … yeah, a little."

"Good, take a seat. Can I get you a glass of water, or some herbal tea, or a soda?"

She glanced at my teacup and scrunched up her face. "I've never cared for tea. You have anything stronger?"

It was ten o'clock in the morning, but given how wound up she was, I had no problem doing whatever was needed to make her comfortable.

"What's your idea of stronger?" I asked. "Coffee?"

"Gin, if you've got it, and if you don't, coffee will have to do."

Gin wasn't something I kept on hand. When I did indulge in spirits, I much preferred vodka. Simone, on the other hand, loved a gin and tonic, and I was sure she wouldn't mind sparing a shot or two for a good cause.

"Let me see what I can find," I said. "I'll be right back."

I found gin, and a variety of other things, in a small cabinet in Simone's office. Poking my head out of her office door, I said, "How do you take it?"

"I'm partial to Negroni's, but I don't expect you have anything to make a cocktail."

"I can make a gin and tonic."

"That works."

I nodded, whipped up her drink and then returned to my desk.

"I heard about Dominic," she said, as I handed her a glass.

"I figured."

She sniffled a few times. "I also heard you were there around the time he … you know … offed himself."

"Who told you?"

"Lenore called me about an hour ago."

"Were you aware she visited Dominic a few times after Noelle died?"

"What do you mean?"

"Dominic told me she stopped by to see him more than once."

"Lenore said she bought him a casserole this morning, and the police were there. One of the neighbors told her they'd overheard Dominic was dead. She'd overheard a cop saying something to another cop about Dominic taking his own life."

"It's funny she brought him another casserole."

"*Another* casserole?"

"Yeah, she took him one yesterday too."

"I wonder why she's been by to see him so many times."

I leaned back, crossing one leg over the other. "Lenore is single, right?"

"Yeah, she is, why?"

"When I saw her at Dominic's house yesterday, I got the feeling she may have been checking in because she was interested in him."

"*Interested* … in a romantic way?"

"Yes."

"How could she even consider such a thing? He'd just lost his wife."

"I don't know," I said. "It was just an observation. Inviting Lenore to your engagement party didn't bother you at all?"

She shrugged. "It didn't. Lucas sees her like a sister now, and she's always been respectful of our relationship. He wanted her to come, so I thought, why not?"

I could think of a few reasons, though I didn't say.

"What happened yesterday, when you went to see Dominic?" she asked.

I paused a moment, considering how much I wanted to say.

"After I was there for a few minutes, Dominic asked Lenore to leave, and we talked for a while," I said. "He wasn't in the best of spirits. At first, he didn't want to talk to me, and then he changed his mind, telling me I could ask him anything I wanted. Why didn't you tell me about the women's center?"

"It didn't come to mind when we spoke the first time."

"Seems to me it's an important detail, one I should have been told about."

"Why?"

"What if the reason she was murdered is tied to the center in some way?"

Zoey raised a brow. "You think so?"

"I do."

"I don't see how it could be. Noelle was careful, not just with the alias she used. To my knowledge, none of the women who came to the center knew much about her personal life, or even where she lived."

Someone knew where she lived, the same someone who wanted her dead.

Zoey went quiet for a moment, then said, "Sorry about … you know, my attitude when you first got here."

"I'm just glad you're in a place where we can talk now. I'm sure hearing about Dominic was unsettling. I'd hoped to tell you myself, but Lenore beat me to it."

"I'm upset about Dominic's suicide, but that's not all. Lucas called off the wedding last night."

"Why? What happened?"

"He's been struggling with the way I've handled Noelle's

death. I'll admit, I haven't been the best person to be around lately."

"I lost someone once, someone who was my entire world, and what I learned is that we all grieve in our own way, in our own time."

"How did you get through it?"

"I quit my job, bought an Airstream, and I went off the grid for a while."

"You seem to have it together now. How did you get past it?"

"I don't think I'll ever get past it, not all the way. I just decided to focus on what I can control instead of what I can't. It will take time. You'll get there."

"It wasn't my intention to push Lucas away the last couple of weeks. I didn't even realize I was doing it."

"Is that what he said—that he felt you'd distanced yourself from him?" I asked.

"Yeah, among other things."

"When you say Lucas called off the wedding, is it temporary? Are the two of you still together?"

"I'm not sure. He said he thought it would be best if we took some time apart. We're living together, but last night, he packed a bunch of his things, and he left. I don't even know where he went. I tried calling, and he didn't answer. He texted me to say he wanted a day to clear his head. I'm trying to give it to him, but it's killing me."

Her erratic outburst earlier made a lot more sense to me now.

First, Noelle was murdered, then Lucas either postponed or canceled the wedding, then he packed a bag and left, and today she learned Dominic was dead too. It would be enough for anyone to break.

Zoey finished off the gin and tonic and dropped the empty cup into the trash. "Why do you think Dominic killed himself? He had a daughter. How could he do that to her after what she's already going through?"

"I got the impression he didn't want to live in a world if Noelle wasn't in it. The way he talked about her when I visited with him made me feel like she meant everything to him. Would you agree?"

"Yes, I would. It was the first thing that came to mind when I heard about what happened, even though I didn't want to believe it. I figured he'd have a rough go of it for a time, but somehow, he'd muddle through and be there for Kiera. I feel so sorry for her. Losing two parents in a month. It's heartbreaking."

My thoughts turned to another question I wanted to ask.

"Do you know a man named Gabe Romero?" I asked.

She blinked at me, shocked at the name I'd just spoken.

Based on her expression, she knew him.

"How do you know about Gabe?" she asked.

"Dominic told me about him, and about what happened when they were in high school. You know about it, right?"

"I know he forced Noelle to have sex after she'd said no. It was a long time before she shared the story with me, but when she did, she told me everything."

"Did you know he was released from prison?"

She nodded. "I guess now would be a good time for me to confess something. Not only do I know he's been out for a while, I went to see him."

"When?"

"Oh, about a week after he was released."

"Did Noelle and Dominic know about your visit?"

"Well, no. I thought it would be best to keep it to myself."

"Why?"

"I didn't want Noelle to be reminded of a past she was trying to forget."

Spoken like a true friend.

"What did you say to him?" I asked.

"My plan was to get in his face, tell him I'd kill him if he ever came anywhere near Noelle again. I had this vision of who I thought he was, an evil, horrible person. And then I saw him face to face, and he was a lot different than I expected."

"In what way?"

"He got super religious in prison. I'm not sure what he was like when Dominic and Noelle knew him, but now he's soft-spoken, and he referred to several different scripture passages during our conversation. When I said Noelle's name, it was like his body went limp. He grabbed the door for support, and then he started crying and saying he was sorry over and over again."

"Do you think it could have all been an act?"

"I've always felt like I can get a good read on people. His behavior, the tears, the remorse, it all seemed genuine to me."

Genuine.

Ted Bundy had been described as genuine in character.

And then he murdered thirty women over a four-year killing spree.

I wasn't buying it.

I was also starting to question all the things she *hadn't* told me during our first meeting. If she wanted justice for her friend, I would have expected her to tell me everything, no matter how irrelevant it may have seemed.

"Don't you think you should have told me about Gabe and the visit you had with him during our first meeting?" I asked.

"I mean, maybe. I guess I don't know why her past with him is relevant. He didn't kill her."

"How can you be so sure?"

"I just am."

"Do you know where he lives?"

"I know where he was living when I went to see him. Not sure where he is now."

It seemed odd to me that Zoey went to see Gabe with the intention of threatening him if he ever tried to see Noelle again. And yet, here she was standing up for him, acting like the rapist was now a saint.

Some people think others can change.

I say, maybe they can, but not *that* much.

"How many people work at the women's center?" I asked.

"I'm not sure. Even though Noelle was passionate about it, she was private when it came to sharing any personal details. It didn't surprise me. She'd always been a private person."

"Is there a specific person who runs the center?"

"Yeah, a woman named Barbara. Not sure about the last name."

Barbara.

I jotted the name down in my notebook.

"I've got another name for you," Zoey said. "I've been going over the conversations I had with Noelle in the weeks before her death, and I remembered something."

"Go on."

"Noelle taught tennis lessons once a week at Royal Palms. She didn't need the money, of course. She did it for the love of the game. A few weeks ago, I picked her up for lunch, and she was upset, which wasn't like her."

"Did she say why?"

"A woman who works at Royal Palms told Noelle she suspected someone working at the club was embezzling money."

"Who was this woman?"

"I'm not sure. Noelle didn't give me a name. I'm guessing she would be someone who knows about the financials of the company."

"Did she tell Noelle who she suspected of stealing money?"

"She did, and Noelle even told me the man's name, but no matter how much I've thought about it, I can't recall it."

"You know it's a man. That's something."

Was it possible Noelle had confronted the man?

If she had, and if she'd said something like he needed to turn himself in or she would do it for him, it was a perfect motive for murder.

Zoey's phone made a dinging sound, and she grabbed it, reading the text message she'd just received. A few seconds later, she shot out of her chair, saying, "I gotta go. Lucas wants to meet."

"Good luck."

"Hey, thanks, I need it. And about earlier … will you apologize to your coworkers for me? I was a bit snippy with them when I first arrived."

I nodded. "Will do."

CHAPTER 13

Simone poked her head inside the door, her eyes darting around.

"You two can come in," I said. "Zoey's gone, and she apologized about her behavior."

Simone breathed a sigh of relief and entered the office.

Hunter followed close behind.

Both ladies walked to my office and sat down.

"So … how did it go?" Simone asked.

"Better than you think. It took some time, but I got her to calm down."

"How?"

"She asked if we had any gin, and I found a bottle in your office. I made her one drink. Hope that's okay."

Simone swished a hand through the air. "Yeah, sure. Whatever works. What was her deal, anyway?"

"She found out about Dominic right before she came here, and she was already having a bad start to her morning. Her fiancé pulled the plug on their wedding last night."

"Why?"

"I get the feeling Zoey's been erratic since Noelle died. I'm sure it's been hard for him to handle. He did text her while she was here, though, and asked to meet, so maybe there's still hope for the two of them."

Hunter nodded, folding her arms as she leaned back in the chair. "Let's talk about the case. What can you tell us about it?"

I told them about the engagement party, the power outage, and Noelle's murder. Then I talked about my visit with Dominic and what we discussed before his suicide.

When I finished, Simone shook her head. "Man, I feel so bad for the child. Both parents dying so close together. How's she doing?"

"I don't know. I've been so busy I haven't had time to check in on her. I'm planning on doing it today."

"Who's the girl with, do you know?"

"Noelle's mother. She lives in town."

"Have you met with Silas about Noelle?"

"I have."

"What did he have to say?"

"He focused on the cause of death. Noelle was manually strangled, and she had fingerprint indentations on her neck, bruises from where she'd been grabbed. He seems to think they're too large to have been made by a woman."

"That's a start," Hunter said.

"What about Foley and Whitlock?" Simone asked. "Do they know we're investigating this case?"

"I spoke with them right after I accepted it."

"Good, now … how can we help?"

I grabbed my notebook, flipping back to the page I needed. I tore it out and set it in front of them. "Here's a list of all the people who were still at the party when the murder took place. Hunter, I'd like you to run a background check on them, see what you can find."

"What about me?" Simone asked.

"Once Hunter gives you their details, I'd like you to speak to them, get their version of what happened that night, so we can see if everyone's stories match up. And, I have something for you." I opened my drawer, pulling out the baggie of photos, and I handed it to her. "Zoey said these photos were taken at the engagement party. I've been through them, and none seem suspicious. As you talk to the party guests, look through the photos. Maybe you'll see something important that I missed."

"Sure thing. Any preference on who I should talk to first?"

I pressed a finger to Lenore's name. "This woman's a curious one."

"How so?"

"She is Zoey's fiancé's ex-girlfriend, so the fact she was even invited to their engagement party seems strange to me. I guess they're still good friends, and Zoey doesn't seem to mind. Even stranger is that Lenore has been stopping by Dominic's house ever since Noelle died."

"What the …? Does she even know the guy?"

"Not well. The first time they met was at the engagement party."

"Then why was she going over there?"

"She said she was checking on him, bringing him a casserole. But from what I understand, there were multiple casseroles delivered."

"Uhh, one casserole I can understand," Simone said. "Multiple? Seems sketchy."

"I think so too."

"What's your opinion about her visits?"

"I think she was interested in Dominic … well, in his money, at least."

Simone and Hunter exchanged glances, and Simone tapped a finger to the top of my desk, thinking. "Silas may be leaning toward a male killer. But what if … and this is a bit of a stretch, but hear me out—what if Lenore showed up to the party, saw the lavish lifestyle Dominic and Noelle were living, and in a moment of jealousy, she murdered Noelle, hoping to step in and cash in on the lifestyle herself?"

"It's a theory, and Lenore is on my radar. I don't think someone would attend a party where they meet the hosts for the first time and make a rash decision to murder the wife in the hopes of assuming their lifestyle. If they'd known each other before, that would be different."

"She was strangled by hand," Simone said, "which tells me her death may have been personal."

"I thought the same thing."

"Do you have any suspects yet?" Hunter asked.

"When I was talking to Dominic, he shared a dark part of Noelle's past. He admitted she was raped in high school by a guy named Gabe Romero, and Hunter, I'd like you to see if you can locate where he's living now so I can pay him a visit. I also want to know about his background and who his parents are."

Hunter grabbed a pen sitting next to my notebook and added his name to the list, along with the words EVIL RAPIST beside it.

"Gabe was Noelle's boyfriend at the time of the rape, which happened when they were at the park one night. He pushed her to have sex, and when she refused, he hit her, and then he raped her. Not long after, Dominic walked by, saw her crying, and that's how their relationship began. He talked her into telling the police about it, and she turned Gabe in."

"Did he serve any time?"

"He did. He pled guilty, went to prison, and he's out now. And here's the strangest part—Zoey just admitted to me that she went to see him after his release. Her original plan, she said, was to threaten him if he ever came near Noelle again, but when she was face to face with him, he was full of humility, like he'd found Jesus and changed his ways. Zoey bought it. She doesn't think he was involved with Noelle's murder."

"What do *you* think?"

"Many sociopaths are skilled in the area of deception. I want to meet this guy and see what I think of him myself. He may have fooled her. He won't fool me."

"I'll see what I can find out about him," Hunter said. "Anything else?"

"I want to know all the names of the staff members at Royal Palms."

"The tennis club? Why?"

"Noelle taught lessons there once a week. During a recent lunch date, Noelle told Zoey she'd heard from one of the female employees that another employee—a male—was embezzling funds."

"Does this woman have a name?"

"Noelle didn't give it."

"What about the man's name?"

"Problem is, Zoey can't remember it."

Simone ran a hand through her hair, shaking her head as she said, "This is a lot to take in. But we're off to a good start with these leads."

"We are, and now it's time we get to work."

CHAPTER 14

"Forgive me for stopping by without calling first," I said. "I was in the neighborhood, and I just wanted to offer my condolences for your daughter and son-in-law."

The woman narrowed her eyes and said, "It's clear you know who I am, but who are you?"

In my anxiousness, I'd managed to skip formal introductions.

I took in a deep breath and tried again.

"I'm sorry if I got ahead of myself just now," I said. "My name is Georgiana Germaine. I was hired by Zoey Morgan to investigate the death of your daughter."

"Ah, yes. Zoey stopped by yesterday. She told me she'd hired someone, but she failed to give me your name."

Noelle's mother looked to be in her late sixties, and she was on the slender side, with long, frizzy, silver hair that cascaded halfway down her back.

I found her stunning.

"I appreciate you taking the time to stop by, but now isn't the best time for a conversation," she said.

I removed a business card from my wallet and handed it to

her. "Before I go, I'd like to leave you my card, so you have my contact information. Call me anytime."

She nodded, and just as she was about to slide the card into her pocket, she hesitated, muttering "Germaine" under her breath.

I wasn't sure why, but I respected her wishes about cutting our visit short, and I nodded and walked away. I was halfway back to my car, when she called out to me, saying, "Miss Germaine, a moment of your time if you don't mind."

I turned back.

"I'm aware you have just taken the case," she said. "Even so, I'd like to know whether you have any leads yet."

"A few."

She glanced at the gold watch on her wrist. "Why don't you come inside? I can spare a few minutes before I pick up Kiera. She's over at my son's house, playing with her cousins. I'm Joanie, by the way."

I followed Joanie to the living room, and we sat on a couple of chairs in front of the fire.

"I understand you went to see Dominic yesterday," she said.

"I did. I was there when he … he, uhh …"

"Yes, it's unfortunate, what happened. He's hasn't been well since Noelle passed. We all knew he was battling depression, but none of us thought it had reached the point where he'd take his own life. I've been made aware of the letter he left. Haven't gotten the chance to see it yet, but Detective Whitlock was kind enough to read it to me over the phone."

"How is Kiera? Is she aware of what happened?"

"Not yet. We haven't decided when to talk to her about it, and we're still working out the healthiest way to have the conversation, not that there is one in this instance. It's never a good time to deliver news of this sort."

"What will happen to her now that both of her parents are gone?"

"In the case events unfolded like they indeed have, Noelle wanted us to take Kiera, and we will, of course. We have a lot of family here, so she'll have a lot of support."

"Have you considered taking Kiera to a therapist?"

Joanie reached for a book, one of many stacked up on the coffee table, and she turned it toward me.

The book was called *The Key to Unlocking a Better Life*.

And the author … Joanie Alldredge.

"I didn't know you were a therapist," I said.

"I've had my practice for almost forty years now. When I saw your name on your business card, I put two and two together, and … let's just say you look a lot like him."

"I look like *him?*"

"Your father, Abe Germaine."

Now I understood why she'd stopped me on my way to my car.

"How did you know my father?" I asked. "Did he come to see you … for, uh, help?"

"He did. Not all the time. When he had a case that was hard for him to deal with, he'd stop in for a chat. He wanted more than anything to keep the stress of his higher-priority investigations to himself, so he didn't bring it home to his family."

"I don't ever remember him talking about his cases much, not unless his coworkers were around."

"He spoke to me about you once, and although it's rather unusual for me to talk about my clients, I don't think he'd mind me sharing something with you."

I leaned in, curious to hear what she had to say. "Go ahead."

"Your father worried you'd follow in his footsteps."

"He worried? Why? I was so young when he passed away."

"As young as you were, you had a genuine interest in his line of work. It reminded him of his own ambitions. He wanted you to have a good life, a happy life, and a career that allowed for those things. Being a detective, even a private eye who works on homicide cases … from what I've learned, it's challenging."

She paused, as if awaiting my response.

"I have a wonderful life, and while my career can be stressful at times, I love what I do," I said. "And while I'm speaking of love, this summer I'm marrying a man I've known since my college years. He's always been supportive of what I do. Sometimes, he even assists with my cases."

She placed a hand on mine. "That's wonderful to hear. If your father was alive today, I'm sure he would be proud."

Wanting to get the subject off of me and back to the case, I said, "If you can spare a few more minutes, I'd like to ask you a few things."

Joanie glanced at her watch once more. "Would you excuse me?"

I nodded, and when she returned a few minutes later, she said, "I've just spoken with my son's wife. She's in no hurry for me to pick Kiera up, so to answer your question … yes, we can continue our discussion."

I was glad to hear it.

"Before we get going on what I'm sure will prove to be a much heavier topic, I have to admit, I'm parched. Would you care for a glass of water?" she asked.

"Sure."

"Lemon, or no?"

"Lemon, thank you."

Joanie went to the kitchen, and it wasn't long before she came back into the room, carrying a tray of two lemon waters and a handful of cookies.

She set it down between us on a circular coffee table.

"It's not often I indulge in sugary treats, but at times like these, I find it's the little things that help us get through," she said. "Please, help yourself."

I grabbed a chocolate chip cookie and a napkin, preparing myself for the difficult topic to come.

"When I was talking to Dominic yesterday, he shared a private part of Noelle's past with me, something they didn't speak of to anyone," I said.

"Are you referring to what happened to Noelle in high school?"

"I am."

"He must have had a good reason for telling you about Gabe."

"I understand now why she opened the Ophelia Albrecht Center."

"Ah, yes. The women's center meant everything to Noelle."

"Did she ever speak to you about any of the women who came to the center?"

"On occasion. It was rare. If she talked to me, it was to get advice. Why do you ask?"

"Even though I've been led to understand she tried to keep her real name and her life private, I'm wondering if someone affiliated with the center discovered her true identity. Perhaps a disgruntled husband whose wife she'd mentored."

"If so, I know nothing about it."

"I heard the police were consulted from time to time, and that in more serious situations, Noelle did what she could to talk some of the women into speaking up about what they'd been through."

"Noelle never pushed. She planted the seed and did what she could to get that seed to grow. It was always the woman's decision to talk to the police, and when they did, if they wished, Noelle remained by their side the entire time."

"Were there any instances when an abuser found out his girlfriend or wife was at the center, and they tried to intervene?"

Joanie gave the question some thought. "It did happen. Not often, but Dominic took precautions right from the start. One of those precautions was hiring security guards—one at the front gate and one as you enter the center. No one comes in or out without checking in, and even then, it's the woman's decision whether or not to see any visitors."

"When you say it's the woman's decision, how does that work?"

"Everyone is stopped at the gate and asked to state their name, which has to be proven by showing the proper identification. The security guard never tells a guest if the woman the person is coming to see is on the premises. He only says he'll check. If a woman refuses a visitor, the visitor is told the woman isn't there."

I was impressed.

"Is there any protection for the women once a visitor gains entry?"

Joanie nodded. "Of course. Staff has a button they can press which lets the security company know there's a problem."

"Has the button ever pressed?"

"To my knowledge, no."

She leaned to the side, grabbing a tissue, and blotting her eyes.

"I know this is hard to talk about," I said.

"It is, you're right, but I am in complete support of what you're trying to do. If talking to me will lead you in the right direction, it will be well worth it."

"Do you remember the last time Noelle asked for your advice about one of the women at the center?"

Joanie reached for a cookie. She took a bite, holding the rest of it in her hand as she said, "Let's see now. There was a recent incident, yes. It's coming back to me now. A woman came to the center. She had a black eye, multiple bruises and wounds."

"Does this type of thing happen often?"

"Not often, no. Many women come to the center seeking refuge after leaving their partners, be it boyfriend, or husband, or otherwise. The center acts as a middle ground. It's the step between shedding their past and healing from their pain as they try to forge a better life for themselves. As for the woman I just mentioned, Noelle convinced her to be looked at by a doctor, but the woman wouldn't admit who'd beaten her."

By law, any doctor who suspected a woman was a victim of domestic violence was mandated by the state to report it.

"I'm assuming the doctor knew she'd been assaulted."

She nodded. "He contacted the proper authorities. Even then, the woman wouldn't give them a name. The police did what they could to try and figure out who'd harmed her, but the woman was unmarried, and she lived alone. When police questioned her coworkers, they confirmed she lived alone. They'd all presumed she was single."

"What happened to the woman?"

"She left the center almost as soon as she arrived, which didn't sit well with my daughter. She admitted to me she'd been to the woman's house, but the woman wasn't there. A day or two went by, and the woman still hadn't been seen, and she hadn't shown up at work. Noelle came to me for advice. She wanted to hire a private investigator."

"Did she?"

"I doubt it. I tried my best to talk her out of it."

"Why?"

"Not knowing the woman's full story, or who harmed her, or why, I was concerned about Noelle's involvement. She'd never put herself at risk in such a way before, not to my knowledge."

So why had she this time?

What was different about this woman than the others?

"Was the woman ever found?" I asked.

"To my knowledge, no."

If Noelle's desire to hire a private investigator hadn't been supported, it was possible she'd hired the investigator and didn't tell anyone.

"How many employees work at the center?" I asked.

"I'm not certain. I can tell you Barbara Adams runs the place. She's been there since the beginning."

Joanie polished off her cookie, washing it down with lemon water, which wasn't to my taste, but to each his own. She reached for another cookie, saying, "Do you have any other questions about the center?"

"None I can think of right now."

"Good, then we should move on. You mentioned Gabe earlier, and I have plenty to say about him."

CHAPTER 15

"Gabe Romero was raised without a mother for the majority of his life," Joanie said. "And his father … well, he wasn't much of one. He was a drunk, and there were times when he was so intoxicated that he abused Gabe. As to the extent of the abuse, I'm not sure."

"How do you know about the abuse?" I asked.

"His drinking problems were common knowledge around town. The abuse didn't come to light until the night Gabe did … well, did what he did to Noelle."

"The night she was assaulted in the park, you mean?"

Joanie nodded. "He'd smacked her around and then … you know the rest—he began apologizing, striking himself in the face, saying he was ashamed. It was then he admitted the abuse he'd suffered. He even lifted his shirt, showing her what he said was proof of the abuse."

"Any chance the bruises were self-inflicted?"

"I can't say, though, knowing the rumors around town back then about his father, I doubt it."

"What happened after Gabe apologized?"

"He begged for Noelle's forgiveness."

"How did she react?"

"She was scared, afraid he'd hurt her again, in the same way or worse. She wouldn't look at him, wouldn't speak to him. He grabbed a knife out of his pocket, held it to his neck, and threatened to kill himself."

I slapped a hand over my mouth. "I wasn't aware. Dominic left that part out."

"I'm not surprised. Dominic never believed any of Gabe's antics were sincere."

"And you? What do you think?"

"I think Gabe was a troubled boy. Trouble or no, it doesn't justify rape."

I agreed.

"What did Noelle do when Gabe threatened to commit suicide?" I asked.

"She asked him to get out of the car."

"And did he?"

"Yes, he apologized a few more times, and then he took off running."

The story I'd been told by Dominic had taken a sharp turn, causing me to wonder what else I didn't know.

"After hearing Zoey and Dominic talk about the type of person Noelle was, I'm surprised she'd ever be interested in a guy like Gabe, even as a teenager. He doesn't strike me as the type of guy she would have dated."

"Teenagers are full of surprises. You have any?"

"I do not. The closest in our family is my niece, Lark. She's almost twelve, and she seems to have her head on straight. I guess we'll see."

"No kids of your own?"

I considered telling her about Fallon, about the accident, about her death, but the truth was, I didn't see any reason why I should.

I shook my head and left it at that.

Joanie broke eye contact, glancing at a nearby wall where several pictures were hanging. I recognized Noelle in a few of them. In every photo, she looked happy and radiant, like a woman living her life to the fullest.

"Noelle was our happy child," she said. "A ball of positive energy. That all changed the night Gabe took her virtue. As a parent, it's hard to forgive, and even harder to forget. If it wasn't for Dominic swooping in when he did, giving her something to live for, heaven knows what would have happened."

"Dominic spoke of his love for Noelle yesterday. What they had seemed special."

"It was, and I worry for Kiera, about how these circumstances will shape her life moving forward."

"She has you and your family."

"You're right, but even with us being a united front, we have a long road ahead."

Joanie grabbed my water glass and hers, taking them to the kitchen for a refill. As I awaited her return, I thought about how impressive she'd been since I'd arrived. She'd managed to keep it together, even though she was suffering a great deal inside.

She returned to the living room, handing one of the glasses of water to me.

"I feel we've veered off the path of the subject we were on," she said.

"The subject of Gabe, you mean?"

"Yes, I gather you consider him a suspect."

"I do, and I'd like to know more about him, from your perspective."

She took some time to gather her thoughts before saying, "Gabe was a broody sort, muscular, and good looking," she said. "Whenever he was in our company, he was quiet, answering my questions with the fewest words possible. He always showed respect to Noelle, but as I assessed his demeanor, I was wary."

"Why?"

"There was something off-putting about him."

"Did you share your feelings with Noelle?"

"Of course, even given how much she liked him, I worried it would be a mistake. I suppose it was because she stopped bringing him around altogether."

"Where did they go if they didn't come here? Knowing what his father was like, it doesn't seem like Gabe would have taken her to his house."

"As far as I know, she never stepped foot in Gabe's house. We forbade it, and Gabe agreed. He didn't trust his father or what he might do if he arrived home drunk and Noelle was there."

"Where did they go, then?"

"They'd meet up at some of the high school joints the kids frequented back then, a few cafes, the movie theater. And at some point, they started going to the park. After she was assaulted, she admitted they'd gone there sometimes, but she swore the most they did was kiss."

Seeing no point in making Joanie relive the pain of what Gabe had done to Noelle, I decided to stick to relationship questions.

"How long did Gabe and Noelle date?" I asked.

"A few months, from what I can remember."

"After she went to the police, I heard he pled guilty."

"You heard right. He did."

"You don't seem surprised."

"I'm not."

"Why?" I asked.

"I mentioned before about Gabe's broody temperament. I should add that he also seemed lost, like he struggled to find purpose in life and didn't expect much out of it. I think that's what attracted him to Noelle. She was his opposite—full of life, always one to lift others up."

Always one to lift others up.

Whether it was someone like Gabe, who had a horrible home

life, and no doubt, little prospects in life, or the women she mentored at the center, her light shone bright until its bitter end …

Until it was snuffed out.

"Did you know Zoey visited Gabe after he was released from prison?" I asked.

Joanie gasped, staring at me in astonishment. "I had no idea. When did this happen?"

"Right after his release."

"Why would she do that?"

"At first, her plan was to tell him to stay away from Noelle. She meant to threaten him."

"What do you mean, *at first*?"

"When I spoke to Zoey this morning, she told me Gabe wasn't anything like she expected him to be. He'd found religion while he served time. When they talked, he kept quoting scriptures."

"How peculiar."

"I agree. It was enough for Zoey to forego her words of warning and to believe Gabe is now a changed man. You knew him. Do you think a man like Gabe is capable of such change?"

She tapped a finger to the cushion of the chair, thinking.

"If I wasn't a therapist, and I was just speaking to you as Noelle's mother, it would be a firm no," she said. "There have been times, not many times, mind you, when someone I've counseled—who I believed couldn't possibly come back from the brink—surprised me."

"I have a hard time believing it myself."

"It wouldn't be possible for me to give you a definitive answer unless the man was standing before me today, though I confess, I have no desire to ever see him again."

She hoped to never see Gabe again, and I, on the other hand, couldn't wait to see him. To witness for myself what had become of him.

"Gabe wrote us a letter," she said.

"When?"

"While he was in prison. He apologized for what he'd done, and he asked for our forgiveness."

"Did you write back?"

"I did not. I thought him undeserving of a response." She stood. "There's something I'd like to show you. Wait here a moment, won't you?"

"Of course."

A couple of minutes later, she sank back down in the chair, her arms wrapped around a shoebox. She pulled the lid off, riffling through it, as she pulled out a few photos.

"After Noelle died, I was going through a few boxes she kept in our garage," she said. "I found several mementos from her high school days. I wasn't aware she'd left them here until my husband told me. We thought it might be nice to open them, go through them together, try to remember the happy times. In doing so, we came across this box, and … well, what was in it."

She handed me several photos.

"Is this Noelle and Gabe?" I asked.

"In happier times, yes."

I scanned them, picking up on a few things.

In each of the photos, Noelle was just as people described her, vibrant and full of life, while Gabe looked solemn, his slight smile looking forced and weighted. And then there were his eyes, menacingly haunting, like he was hiding something.

"Can I keep these?" I asked.

"Sure, I was going to cut him out of them and toss his half in the trash."

"I can bring them back if you'd like."

"Oh, it's all right. We have a lifetime of photos of her."

I stood, thanking her for talking with me, and she accompanied me to the front door. I turned, asking one final question.

"After all these years, do you think Gabe could be responsible for Noelle's murder?" I asked.

"As much as it pains me to think about what he did to Noelle, I do not. What purpose would he have in doing so?"

I wasn't sure of the purpose myself.

It didn't mean he didn't have one.

If he did, I was about to find out.

CHAPTER 16

During my visit with Noelle's mother, Hunter had messaged me with Gabe's address. He lived in Arroyo Grande, a sleepy little village steeped in rich history. With a population of less than twenty thousand, it was known for its coastal views and historic swinging bridge. And, of course, its roosters, which could often be seen roaming the village streets.

Gabe's current residence was a bright-blue, double-wide mobile home. After I parked on a patch of loose gravel, I walked up the front steps, leading me to a porch with a metal overhang spanning the width of the home. The front door was ajar, with the exception of several strands of long, wooden beads dangling across its opening.

Inside the home, guided meditation streamed through speakers, the woman speaking about mindfulness and remembering to be in the present moment.

I cupped a hand to the side of my mouth and shouted, "Hello? Gabe?"

When no response came, I pushed the beads to the side, poking my head through the doorway, my eyes coming to rest on

Gabe. He was dressed in a T-shirt and shorts, sitting on the floor in front of a worn leather sofa, his eyes closed, legs crossed.

He was a lot smaller than I imagined he'd be, about half the weight of the teenager I'd seen in the pictures. His slender frame was bony in areas, almost to the point of malnourishment.

I raised my voice and tried getting his attention a second time, which proved successful.

His eyes flashed open, and he reached for a remote control sitting beside him, silencing the meditation session.

"Can I help you?" he asked.

"I hope so. My name is Georgiana Germaine. I am a private detective, and I was hoping to ask you a few questions."

"I don't mind answering your questions, but why have you come to speak with me?"

"I've been hired to look into the death of Noelle Winters."

Eyes wide, he ran a hand across his mouth, his expression shifting to sadness. "Noelle Alldredge, do you mean?"

"Alldredge was her maiden name, yes."

He pushed himself off the floor, coming to a standing position. "Please … please, come in."

I nodded and stepped inside.

He took a seat on the sofa and offered for me to do the same.

I remained standing, close to the door, for a variety of reasons —one being my fear that the '40s color block, collared dress I was wearing would fall victim to one of the plethora of visible couch stains.

"Are you aware Noelle died?" I asked.

"Not at all. When did she pass away?"

"A couple of weeks ago."

"What happened, if you don't mind me asking?"

"I do not. She was murdered."

His jaw dropped open. "She was *murdered?*"

"At an engagement party she was hosting, yes. In the middle

of the party, there was a power outage, and during that time, she was strangled to death."

His eyes began to water, and he bowed his head, voice lowering to a shaky rattle. "Of all the people who didn't deserve something like that to happen, she'd be at the top."

"Why do you say that?"

"Noelle showed me kindness when no one else did, kindness I didn't deserve and still don't." He paused, then added, "She opens her mouth with wisdom, and the teaching of kindness is on her tongue."

And just like that, the scripture-quoting part of our conversation had commenced.

I feigned innocence, for now, saying, "I'm not sure what you mean."

"Proverbs 31:26."

"I see."

"Are you a religious woman, Miss Germaine?"

I ignored the question.

What I was or was not was none of his concern, nor did it have any relevance to the reason for my visit.

"I'd like to see your hands, if you don't mind," I said.

"Of course, may I ask why?"

"I've seen the autopsy photos. There were bruises on Noelle's neck, finger impressions from being strangled."

"If you've come here today to find out if I had anything to do with her murder, let me put you at ease. I did not. I haven't seen Noelle since we were in court."

He raised his hands in front of him like he was under arrest, and I stepped forward. For as slender as he was, his fingers were large.

"Satisfied?" he asked.

"I'm not, but you can put your hands down now."

I stared at him for a moment, and he stared back, and I noticed something I hadn't in the photos I'd seen—his eyes were two different colors. One brown, the other more yellowish-green. It was a rare condition called heterochromia, affecting a mere 1% of the population.

He placed his hands in his lap and turned, looking out the window at a large pine tree. "I'm sorry to hear about her death, and I hope her family is all right. Her parents are good people, even if they hate me, as I imagine they still do. Hatred stirs up strife, but love covers all wrongs."

"If you don't mind, can we forego the scripture passages during our visit?"

He shrugged. "I didn't mean to offend."

"You haven't offended, but let's stick to discussing the topic at hand."

"The topic of murder, you mean."

"I do. Where were you on the evening of March 13th?"

"Hard for me to remember what I did yesterday, let alone where I was over two weeks ago."

"Try."

"I don't get out much. I find it's better to keep to myself. Helps my head to remain clear, free of things I ought not to think about."

"Can you answer the question?"

"I'd say I was home that evening, as I am most evenings."

"Alone?" I asked.

"Yes, ma'am."

"I've learned a lot about you today, about your home life in your younger years, your father, the night you assaulted and raped Noelle."

He closed his eyes. "I'm trying to engage in conversation with you, to answer any questions you've come to ask, but you're making it hard."

"I'm just stating the facts."

He opened his eyes, and even though I didn't want to admit it, those same eyes, the ones I'd seen in the photos, so dark, so menacing, had somehow changed. They were much softer now.

"As I was saying, I do everything I can to keep my mind clear, in the present where it belongs, and not in the past," he said. "Nothing positive will come from dragging up unpleasant memories."

"I understand, and I hope *you* understand I have a job to do."

"I suppose me telling you I'm innocent isn't enough, is it?"

"I'm sorry to say it isn't. Not yet."

"I look forward to the day you're sure of my innocence. Is there anything else I can answer for you?"

"I have some questions about your father."

"What about him?"

"Is he still alive?"

"As far as I know, he's still around, though I'm surprised the alcohol hasn't gotten the better of him by now. I can't imagine he's kicked the habit. Don't see why he ever would."

"Do you see him?"

"Not since the day I was arrested."

"Why not?"

"I thought it best to cut him out of my life. With him in it, there's no chance for me to be a better person, to be the man I work day and night to be."

"And what kind of man is that?"

"A humble one, a man who seeks to better himself and the world around him, so that one day, when I die, I may be forgiven for my past sins."

He was either doing a superb job of acting, or he had become the one person I didn't believe he could—a changed man.

"Since your release from prison, what have you been doing?" I asked.

"I live a modest life." He got up and walked to the kitchen. "I'd like to show you something."

On the off chance he couldn't be trusted, I dipped my hand inside my bag, palming my gun.

He opened a kitchen cabinet and pulled out a tray full of handmade soap, a bit of glitter spilling off the tray in the process. "There's a local craft market up the road. I have a booth there each week on Saturday. Sell out just about every time. You ever been to Crafty Couture on Main Street?"

"I haven't."

"My soap is sold there too."

"How did you get into soap making?"

"I read a book about it when I was locked up. I thought it would be something I'd enjoy doing, and I was right. Been making soap ever since I got my own place."

"Does it pay your bills?"

"Can't say I have many of those. The trailer belonged to my aunt, my mother's sister. While I was serving time, she married a wealthy man, and she wrote to me to say she was deeding this place to me. I sure am grateful. As for other expenses, I don't have a car, but I do have a bike. It's kinda crazy how cheap you can live if you're not afraid to give up a few luxuries."

He grabbed a shimmery pink bar of soap off the tray. The bar had a sliver of black running through the middle. He slipped it into a small white bag and walked over to me. "Here, I'd like you to have one."

"Oh, I don't think it's a good idea for me to—"

"Please, it's yours."

"How about you allow me to pay you for it?"

He swished a hand through the air. "Don't bother."

Against my better judgment, I accepted the bar and changed the subject.

"Do you have a girlfriend, or are you dating anyone?" I asked.

He returned to the sofa, shaking his head as he sat down. "I haven't dated a woman since my release."

"Why not?"

"I don't trust myself, I guess."

"I thought you were trying to live in the present and to leave the past behind."

"It's true, I am. I suppose the thing that scares me the most is having to tell another woman about the mistakes I've made. It wouldn't be right not to tell her, but once I did, I couldn't see any woman sticking around after that. Even though I've changed, I'd still be seen as a monster, and the truth is, I was one, but I'm not one now."

I had mixed feelings about what he'd just said, and now I understood why Zoey felt the way she did when they'd met. Standing in front of him now, I found myself wanting to forgive his past transgressions, even though I was conflicted. Part of me was of the mind that he didn't warrant forgiveness, no matter how much he'd changed.

"Do you have any friends?" I asked.

"A few."

"Are they aware of your past?"

He nodded. "They're part of my church group."

The sound of a vehicle rolling to a stop out front distracted me from the conversation, and I turned.

Gabe stood, peering out the window, and said, "Guess I'm a popular guy today. Wonder who those two are?"

CHAPTER 17

"The man on the left is Chief Foley, and the man on the right is Detective Whitlock," I said.

"Friends of yours, I imagine?"

"They are."

Whitlock approached the beaded doorway and stood there a moment, as if he wasn't sure what to do about it. Then he leaned to the side, tapping his knuckle to the window as he announced himself.

"You can both come in," Gabe said.

They entered the home, and Whitlock smiled at me, saying, "Fancy meeting you here, Georgiana. Great minds think alike."

"That they do."

Foley tipped his head toward me and said, "Have you been here long?"

"A little while. I figured you both would've beat me to it." I glanced at the clock on the wall. "I should get going, leave you both to question him yourselves."

"You might want to stay."

Whitlock nodded in agreement, and I realized I was about to be let in on something I didn't yet know.

"We've just done another sweep of Dominic and Noelle's home, and we found something we'd like to talk to you about, Gabe," Whitlock said.

"All right," Gabe said.

Whitlock reached into his pocket, producing what appeared to be a letter.

"We didn't see it the first time we went through the house because it was stuck to the underside of the lamp on Noelle's nightstand."

"We're thinking she may have put it there intentionally," Foley said, "to perhaps hide it from her husband."

"If she was hiding it, why wouldn't she just throw it away?" I asked.

"Given Noelle and Dominic are both dead, I guess we'll never know."

"Who's Dominic?" Gabe asked.

"Noelle's husband," I said.

"He's dead, too?" Gabe said. "Strangled?"

"Not strangled," I said. "After Noelle died, he killed himself."

Gabe slapped a hand to his lips, his head shaking. "Oh, this is awful. So, so, so awful."

"What we want to know is … when did you write her this letter, and why?" Foley asked.

"Sure, I'll tell you," Gabe said. "I'll tell you everything."

"Hold on a minute," I said. "May I see the letter so I can get up to speed on what's happening here?"

Whitlock looked at Foley, who nodded, and passed the letter to me.

I opened it and began to read.

Dear Noelle,

I can't thank you enough for your letter and for reaching out to me after all this time, and I want you to know how much your kind words mean to me. I've thought a lot about you over the years, wondering how you are and what your life might be like, as I hoped for every happiness for you and your family.

If it wasn't for my concern about stirring up the past, I would have made contact as soon as I was released. There are so many things I've wanted to say to you.

First, no amount of apologies I could ever give could make up for that awful night. I pushed you to do something, even after you asked me to stop, and for that, I will never forgive myself. The best thing I could do was to learn from my mistakes, and learn I have.

While I was serving my time, I found great comfort in the scriptures. Up to that point, I'd never considered myself a spiritual person. I was more of an atheist, if anything. But something about the many passages I read spoke to me, and I found the more I relied on the words, the more I began to feel real change.

Some people don't believe others can change, and that's all right. But I want you to know that I have changed, and I promise you, I am a better man, a humble man. And I will never harm anyone again.

I hope that you are living your best life, your fullest life, and that you've been able to shed the past, becoming the brilliant woman I've always known you to be.

Gabe Romero

P.S. I'd like to close with a scripture, one that holds great meaning to me:

Be sorry for your sins and cry because of them. Be sad and do not laugh. Let your joy be turned to sorrow. Let yourself be brought low before the Lord. Then He will lift you up and help you. – James 4:9-10

I handed the letter back to Whitlock and turned toward Gabe. "You made no mention of this letter to me. Why not?"

"I wasn't trying to keep it from you, or any of you. When you told me she was murdered, I thought it might be best if I kept it to myself."

"Because if you told me, you figured it would make you look like a prime suspect in her murder."

"It's one of things that crossed my mind, yes. If I didn't murder her, and I did not, I didn't see any relevance in discussing the letter."

"By not discussing it, you've made yourself look even guiltier," Foley said. "Didn't think of that—now, did you?"

"I understand how it looks, but I swear to you, whatever happened to Noelle had nothing to do with me."

Foley and Whitlock exchanged glances, like they were questioning everything.

So was I.

"Let's back up a minute," I said. "In your letter you thanked Noelle for reaching out, and you mentioned a letter she wrote to you. Do you have it?"

"That was my next question," Foley said.

Gabe nodded. "Of course I have it."

He walked to a bedroom, and I heard him shuffling around. Then he returned, holding the letter out as he said, "Who should I give this to first?"

Foley held out a hand.

He opened the letter, looked it over, and then handed the letter and the envelope to Whitlock. Whitlock did the same and then handed it to me, making me wonder why they hadn't just read it aloud instead of playing a game of "pass the letter."

The letter said:

Gabe,

After all this time, I never thought I'd find myself sitting at my desk, writing you a letter. When you were first released from prison, I'll admit I had a fair amount of trepidation, even though I didn't believe any further harm would come to me. I can't explain it, but it was there, a worrisome feeling that sent me back to the night you forced yourself upon me.

To get past my feelings, I decided to seek out a therapist, and it was in those sessions that I felt a greater sense of healing and a better understanding of the person you were back then. Even though you did what you did, there was another side of you, a side I saw that most didn't ... a goodness if only you could conquer the demons of your upbringing and seek after a better life.

Your father raped your mother, and you, in turn, raped me. As you sat in the car with me that night, sobbing and telling me the horrors you'd endured at the hand of your father, I felt for you, even though I thought I shouldn't have.

I want to explain why I did what I did, confessing the rape to the police, which led to your arrest and incarceration. The one thing you needed more than anything was to get away from your father and putting you behind bars was a way to accomplish just that.

I hoped in the years you served that you could become your own man, a man who could step out of his father's shadow and become the man you wanted to be.

I want you to know that I forgive you, and I hope you've forgiven yourself. And I hope you are seeking a better life than the one you lived before.

Noelle

I placed the letter back into the envelope, flipping it over to see the date it was postmarked.

"She sent you this letter a month before she was murdered," I said.

"I know," Gabe said, "which is why not telling you about it seemed like a good idea. Look, it's easy to convict the felon, a lot easier than pinning her murder on someone else. I'm willing to do whatever it takes to convince you, be it a polygraph or whatever else."

"Noelle lived a private life over the past several years," I said. "So, what I'm wondering is, how did you find her address? It's not listed on the outside of this letter."

"You're right. I tried everything I could think of to find an address for her once I'd written my response. I couldn't find anything, and I didn't know her surname. I assumed her parents still lived in the same house, but I didn't dare send it there."

"Why not?" Foley asked.

"I was sure they wouldn't give it to her, and also, I thought they might read it. If they did, they would have known she'd sent a letter to me, and I thought that was information she might not want them to have."

"You still haven't answered the question. You got the letter to her somehow."

"When her friend Zoey visited me, she said a few things about herself during the visit, which made her easier to find. I do not choose to engage in any kind of social media online, but one of the men in my church group does, and his father was in law enforcement. It took all of ten minutes to find Zoey online, and then once we figured out her last name, the rest was easy."

"So you wrote to Zoey, and what, asked her to give Noelle your letter?" I asked.

"I did, and I never knew if she had done it—not until now."

"When did you send the letter to Noelle?" Foley asked.

"A week after I received her letter."

"A couple weeks before she was murdered."

Gabe nodded.

Foley raised a hand. "I've heard enough for now. Gabe, I'd like you to come down to the department, and we'll continue this conversation there."

"Am I under arrest?"

"Not yet."

Gabe grabbed a hoodie off the arm of the couch.

The four of us headed for the door, and Foley turned toward me.

"I'd like for us to speak to him alone," he said.

"Meaning, you don't want me in the room when you question him."

"Correct. But we should catch up soon and compare notes."

I shot him a wink and said, "Oh, don't worry. We will."

CHAPTER 18

It was dinnertime when I arrived back in Cambria, but before I retired for the night, I had one more stop to make. And since Giovanni was away, there was no rush to get home, though I imagined our furry friend was missing us both.

I turned into the parking lot at the Royal Palms Tennis Club, taking a moment to admire the stark-white grandeur of the club's massive building before I exited the car. It was impressive, giving off an air of wealth and status. Reaching for my phone, I pulled up a text message Hunter had sent me, listing the names of the club's staff members.

Looking over the list, the most likely woman who'd talked to Noelle about the possible fraud taking place at the club was Annie Jackson in the accounting department.

I entered the club and made my way to the reception desk. A spunky teen with blond pigtails dressed in a fitted, long-sleeved shirt and a tennis skirt blinked at me and smiled. "Hi, welcome. Can I help you?"

"I'm looking for Annie Jackson. I believe she works in accounting."

"Annie, yeah."

"Is she here?"

The girl leaned to the side, glancing down the hallway. "Umm, I don't know. Wait here, and I'll check."

The girl bounced her way in the opposite direction, entering an office down the hall. Staring through the office window, I could see she hadn't gone to find Annie for me. Instead, she was talking to a man. I wondered why.

The man looked to be close to my age, and he was tall and fit, his arm muscles bulging out of the polo shirt he was wearing.

He turned toward me, narrowing his eyes.

Then he advanced in my direction.

The spunky teen stayed behind.

"What can I do to help you?" he asked.

"I'm here to see Annie. I'm not sure why the girl from reception got you instead."

"I'm Clark Fletcher, the manager. Who are you? And what's your business with Annie?"

Given his curt tone, I had a feeling announcing myself and my intentions for being there wasn't a good idea, but he'd put me on the spot.

"I was friends with Noelle Winters," I said. "Before she died, I expressed an interest in becoming a member of the club and taking up tennis lessons. She was going to teach me, but now that she's gone, I was hoping I might be able to take lessons from someone else."

He crossed his arms. "What does that have to do with Annie?"

"Noelle and Annie were friends, and I thought Annie might be able to give me advice on who I should take lessons from now that Noelle is … well, now that she's passed away."

"Annie doesn't mingle much with our tennis instructors."

"She mingled with Noelle, didn't she?"

A door opened down the hall, and a woman poked her head out, blinking in our direction. Given Clark's back was to her, he hadn't noticed yet. The woman was on the shorter, stockier side, and she was older, in her early seventies, I guessed. Her long, salt-and-pepper hair was braided on both sides.

Clark cocked his head to the side, eyeing me in such a way that told me he wasn't buying my reason for being there. "You look familiar."

"It's a small town."

"Yes, it is, but where have I seen you before?"

"I'm not sure. I don't believe we've ever met."

"Not in person, but …" he paused, then raised a finger. "Ah, I know where I've seen you. It was in the newspaper."

"I can't remember the last time I was in the newspaper."

"It was an article about a local detective solving yet another murder. The detective was you. Now, why don't you tell me the real reason for your visit?"

"I've already told you."

"I don't believe you're telling me the truth, and I don't believe you're interested in lessons either. If I had to guess, someone's hired you. Given the police haven't solved the case yet, it makes sense. Doesn't it?"

"Can't a private detective also have an interest in tennis lessons?"

"Are you saying you *weren't* hired to investigate Noelle's murder?"

At this point, there was no reason to keep up the ruse any longer.

"You're right. I was hired."

"Why are you here? And I'd appreciate it if you'd tell me the real reason this time, if you don't mind."

"I know Noelle taught lessons here when she was alive, and I thought it might be helpful to talk to some of her friends, starting with Annie. I also thought Annie would know who else had a relationship with her."

"The police have already been here. They've made their inquiries, and we complied with all their requests. If you're planning to do the same, and it sounds like you are, coming here is a waste of your time."

"Why's that?"

"No one here had anything to do with Noelle's unfortunate death."

"To your knowledge. Besides, I didn't imply that they did. I'm trying to get a better picture of who Noelle was, including her friends."

He shook his head, sighing. "I see no need to continue this conversation any further. I'd like you to leave."

He lifted a finger, pointing at the door.

Feeling defeated, I was disappointed in myself and how I'd handled things. I should have given more thought to the visit, had better responses to his questions, a backup plan for the backup plan. Now, being left with no choice other than to leave without accomplishing what I'd intended, I decided it best to regroup, come at it again another day with another angle.

I made my way to my car, stopping when I heard the sound of brisk footsteps fast approaching. As I turned, I saw the woman who'd poked her head out of her office door. She had a hand pressed to her chest, panting like she was out of breath.

"I'm Annie," she said. "Why did you ask to see me?"

And just like that, it seemed I *had* accomplished something after all.

"I wanted to talk to you about a conversation I believe you may have had with Noelle a few weeks before she died."

Annie looked around, nervous. "We can talk, but not here."

"When do you get off work?"

"My shift ended ten minutes ago. I still have a few things to do before I leave for the day."

I reached into my bag, pulling out a business card. "We can meet at my office when you're ready."

Annie accepted the card, nodding as she said, "Give me thirty minutes, and I'll be there."

CHAPTER 19

At thirty minutes on the dot, Annie entered my office, her expression one of worry as she made her way toward me. I suggested we take a seat on the sofa, and we did.

"This entire thing is such a mess," she blurted. "I don't know what to make of it."

"You don't know what to make of what?"

"After you left the tennis club, Clark pulled us all aside. He told us you'd been hired to investigate Noelle's murder. Then he said he didn't want us talking to you."

And yet, she was here, doing what she'd been asked *not* to do.

"Clark can't tell any of you who to talk to or not talk to," I said. "You're here, and I'm assuming it's because there's something you need to get off your chest."

"I'm here because I don't have a choice. When you came to my place of work, asking for me by name, I figured if you didn't talk to me there, you'd find another way to do it."

"Do you know *why* I asked to see you?"

Annie leaned back, crossing her arms. "I think so, yes, though if you know what I think you do, it means Noelle spoke of the private conversation we had with someone else. What I told her was in confidence, to a friend I thought I could trust."

"From everything I've learned about Noelle, she was worthy of your trust. I believe she spoke to a friend because she was seeking advice on what to do with the information you gave her."

"Still, I don't like it. Things have a way of getting around in this town. What did this *friend* tell you about my conversation with Noelle?"

I thought about whether it would be best to divulge the conversation, as it had been relayed to me, or whether it would be best to feed her bits and pieces first to gauge her response.

"I should start by saying Noelle's friend is the person who hired me," I said. "A few weeks before Noelle died, she had lunch with this friend, and she mentioned a woman at Royal Palms had come to her and shared some sensitive information. The woman believed a man working at the club had been committing fraud. I'm going to get right to the point. You suspected someone at Royal Palms was committing fraud, correct?"

Annie pressed her hands together. "Do I have to answer the question?"

"You don't *have* to do anything, though it would make my job a lot easier if you did. You should know, I'm good at my job. The truth will come out, one way or another."

She huffed an irritated, "Fine. I've been carrying the weight of what I suspect is going on at the club for months now. I tried to keep it to myself, and for a while, I did. Then I got to a point where the weight of it was so heavy, I thought if I didn't talk about it to someone, I'd have a complete meltdown."

"It makes sense. Keeping a secret like the one you've been keeping is never easy. Why did you decide to confide in Noelle?"

"She was my closest friend at the club, and I figured she'd offer me some good advice. I just didn't expect her to be so upset about what I told her. She'd always been so levelheaded. When she reacted the way she did, part of me regretted saying something. If it all came out, and I was wrong about my suspicions, I would have lost my job."

"You can always get another job. And hey, you're still alive. The same can't be said for Noelle."

Annie bowed her head, voice lowered as she said, "Do you think it's possible someone at the club murdered Noelle?"

"I don't know yet. I don't even know whether she was killed by a male or a female. But I will figure out what happened to her and why."

Given Annie had strong-looking hands, she was an easy suspect. She'd also been harboring a secret, one she was worried might come out before she was ready to reveal it. Seemed like a motive for murder to me.

Upon hearing me say I suspected the killer could be of either gender, Annie gasped. "You think a *woman* could have murdered Noelle?"

"I'm open to the possibility."

"Huh, I wouldn't think a woman would strangle a person to death, not when there are so many easier ways to kill someone."

It was such a peculiar thing to say.

"What method would you consider *easy*?" I asked.

She gave the question some thought, shrugged, and said, "Poison, I guess."

She was right and she was wrong at the same time.

Poisoning as a murder method was used by women in 4% of their cases and by men in just 1%, accounting for only 0.5% of all murders overall.

"In Noelle's case, it isn't *how* she was murdered that matters," I said. "I care more about statistics. In women, murder is often personal. Over 75% are killed by someone they know."

"Wow, I had no idea. You said you don't know who did it, but do you have any suspects yet?"

She was getting ahead of herself, making me feel like I was being steered in another direction, one where she spared herself from telling me what she'd told Noelle. I wasn't about to let that happen.

"I have a few suspects," I said, "which brings me back to the tennis club."

"I must admit, I've been fraught with worry, wondering if something I shared with Noelle in confidence could in some way be related to her death."

"I think you should assume it could be, which is why I need to know everything. If someone is stealing money from the club and that person found out Noelle knew about it, she could have been killed to keep the truth from coming out."

Annie went silent, her hands shaking. "What if he did find out she knew, and what if he finds out the information came from me? It's enough to make me want to forget this whole business, forget I know anything about it."

"I know you're afraid," I said. "And even though you might have some regrets about telling Noelle, something inside you knew you needed to do it, that it was the right thing to do."

"I thought I could confide in her, and she'd keep my secret until I could prove it. Seems that's not what happened."

"What *did* happen?"

There was a long pause. "Oh, all right. I suppose there's no getting out of it now, is there? Here's what I know. A little over a year ago, a man who'd worked in accounting for over twenty years decided to retire. Clark started interviewing potential replacements, and then out of nowhere, he hired Owen Beaumont, a guy who'd been working in client services."

"Did Owen have any experience in finance?"

"He said he went to school for accounting, but I'm not sure Clark ever took the time to check and see whether he was telling the truth or not."

"Clark strikes me as a guy who would vet a person, even if that person already worked there."

"You're right. Here's the catch. Owen's uncle is the biggest shareholder of the tennis club, meaning, what he says goes. He made it clear to Clark that he wanted Owen moved to a position where he could earn more money. Once Owen had the new job, it wasn't long before Clark noticed Owen was overwhelmed, but he knew he'd face backlash over removing Owen from the position. That's where I came in."

"How long did Owen work in accounting before you were hired?"

"About nine months. I was brought on to be his part-time assistant, even though I could do in two hours what he couldn't do in eight."

"What's it like, working with Owen?"

"We got off on the wrong foot, for starters. He didn't want me there, and he wasn't happy when Clark decided he needed help. I tried to build a bridge between us. I was nice; I brought in cookies. It didn't matter. Owen wanted nothing to do with me."

"How did he behave toward you?"

"Owen was distant and secretive. He'd give me menial tasks, never anything too big or too personal. He oversaw most of the financial transactions and handled all the banking. I process employee paychecks and take care of client dues."

"Tell me how you came to suspect he was mismanaging money."

Annie closed her eyes, nodding. "It started with me worrying Owen wasn't doing his job. If Clark was out of the office for the day, Owen would show up late for work, or he'd leave early. He was on salary, and given the power his uncle had, he must have thought no one would tattle, and he was right. No one dared say a thing."

"Were you doing any of his work for him during that time?"

"He told me not to, but I couldn't help myself. One day, I decided to have a wee look-see at his bookkeeping to make sure things weren't getting behind. My concern was that Owen would point the finger at me for any issues about the books."

"When you looked through things, what did you find out?"

"Well," she said, leaning toward me, "the books were a mess. I couldn't make heads or tails of the deposits. Nothing added up, no matter how many times I tried to balance it all."

"Did you say anything to him?"

"Given he'd forbidden me from looking at the books, I was afraid to ask him about it."

"Was Clark aware Owen kept you from certain aspects of the job?"

"If he was, he never said anything to me, and given I'm one of the newer hires, I didn't know if I could trust him with that information."

Annie's stomach grumbled, and I turned, looking out the window. I hadn't realized how dark it had gotten in the time we'd been chatting. I was sure she was on the verge of a bombshell confession, and I didn't want her to leave—not yet.

CHAPTER 20

"Are you hungry?" I asked.

"I'm starving," Annie said.

While the kitchen was not always stocked with food—at least none filling enough to be considered a meal—I always kept a variety of cheeses on hand.

I stood and said, "Come with me."

We walked to the kitchen, and I opened the refrigerator, assessing our options. Pulling out a few different blocks of cheese and some grapes, I then grabbed some nuts and crackers out of a cabinet. I looked to her for approval and was given an enthusiastic thumbs-up.

I laid the snacks out on a tray, grabbed a couple of plates, and invited her to get whatever she wanted to drink out of the refrigerator. Then we took it all to the table. It was my favorite spot in the office, given it was adjacent to a soothing, floor-to-ceiling wall fountain Giovanni had gifted me to celebrate the opening of the detective agency.

"Don't you have anywhere to be tonight?" Annie asked.

"No, although I'm sure my dog is wondering what's become of me, so I won't keep you much longer. I didn't want you to leave before you could say everything you came to say, and I don't think you have."

"You're right, there's more."

"Why don't we have a bite to eat, and then we'll finish our conversation about Owen afterward?"

For the next few minutes, we chatted about lighter topics. She asked me how I got started in the business and how long I'd lived in Cambria. We talked about her life and her friendship with Noelle. She seemed to be in better spirits, and I hoped it would get her to the finish line.

I popped the last of the cheese slices into my mouth, pushing my plate to the side. "The more you've told me, the more I'm convinced you wouldn't have approached Noelle about Owen unless you had evidence to back up your story."

I crossed my arms, waiting for her response.

It took some time before she offered it.

And though I was tiring to the point my eyelids began to feel heavy, I waited, trying my best not to push.

"If I level with you, telling you what I know, what's going to happen?" she asked.

"I don't think you're asking the right question."

"What would the right question be?"

"An innocent life has been taken. What's it worth to you?"

"It's worth a lot. Noelle was a good friend. I'll be honest—ever since she died, I've been having a hard time sleeping."

I assumed the lack of sleep wasn't just over Noelle's death, but also over the fear that if Noelle died because of what Annie had told her, maybe she was next.

"Do you think your lack of sleep is because you feel guilty?" I asked.

"It's part of it."

"You don't have anything to feel guilty for, Annie. You did the right thing. Maybe confessing what you haven't yet will help. You don't want to live the rest of your life asking yourself who murdered Noelle and why, so help me find her killer."

"It's all heavy … too heavy. I want nothing more than to put it all behind me and move on."

"I want that for you too."

Annie placed her plate on top of mine and took a sip of water.

Wiping her mouth with a napkin, she said, "Here it is, and what I suspect you already know … I believe Owen has been using some of the club's money as his own personal bank account."

"In what way?"

"Several checks have been torn out of the checkbook without the carbon copy to say who those checks were written to and why."

"If he's stealing company funds, it seems logical he's been writing checks to himself and then cashing them. Would you agree?"

"I would."

"How long do you suspect he's been doing it?" I asked.

"Since he took over the position. It wasn't a daily occurrence, though. I suspected once or twice a month at first. Then I think he got comfortable, assumed he was getting away with it—and that he could keep getting away with it."

"Did the number of missing checks increase?"

"They did. Once or twice a month turned into once a week, or more. I'm not sure how much he's taken in total. I don't have access to the company's bank account."

I considered all she'd told me so far.

It was good information, the strongest lead I had in the case.

If I was going to nail someone for embezzlement, and for murder, I needed to be sure I had the right person.

"How do you know Owen stole the money and not someone else who works there?" I asked.

"For one, the longer we've worked together, the more accessories he seems to own, accessories he didn't wear to work at the start. The most notable is a watch. He never wore watches to work at the start of my job, and then one day, he started wearing the same one every day. One time, I got close enough to get a good look at it."

"Were you able to identify the brand?"

"Yes, Cartier. I looked it up online. It sells for over seven thousand dollars!"

"If Owen's uncle is the main investor in the club, I'm assuming he has money."

"Oh, yeah. He's loaded. We're talking millions."

"Wouldn't the rest of the family benefit from his millions?"

Annie laughed, saying, "Owen had a nickname for his uncle—*The Grinch.* He said his uncle believed everyone needed to find their own way. He was willing to give people in the family an opportunity to work their way up, but he believed they had to start at the bottom, proving themselves first."

"Do you happen to know his uncle's name?"

"It's a name you can't forget—Alexander Beaumont."

A fitting name, indeed.

I reached for a pen, scribbling the name in my notebook.

"Aside from Owen wearing flashy jewelry, is there any other proof you have that he was stealing company money?" I asked.

"I caught him once … well, that is to say, I walked in on him when he was tearing one of the checks out of the book—*a blank check.* There's no doubt I'd caught him off guard. He thought I was at lunch, because I'd told him as much. My plan was to circle back to say I'd forgotten my purse, see if anything nefarious was going on, and it worked."

"What did Owen do when he saw you?"

"He made a strange comment about how he'd torn the check out to reimburse one of our clients who'd canceled their membership and complained they were still being charged dues. I knew of no such client, and even if what he said were true, it would have been my job to sort it out, not his."

"My guess is Owen didn't know what else to say in the moment, so he told you the first thing that sprung to mind. How did you respond?"

"I offered to handle the client myself so he didn't have to bother with it. He gave me a firm no, and I didn't press it any further. Ever since, Owen has been far more careful."

As expected.

"Any embezzler, even one who isn't smart, knows enough to not leave an evidence trail," I said. "You said there were missing checks, but unless he's a complete imbecile, and maybe he is, I imagine he would have gone to great lengths to cover his tracks after you caught him red-handed with a blank check."

She nodded. "You're right. I believe he's hidden or destroyed any evidence about what he's been doing."

"How do you know?"

"I haven't seen the checkbook for a while, or the book containing the company bank statements. Can't find them anywhere in the office, and believe me, I've looked."

"When you went to Noelle about what you thought was happening, I'm guessing she tried to get you to do the right thing and report him."

"She did. She encouraged me to talk to Clark about my suspicions. I said no. It's like I said before, I don't know him well enough to know how aligned he is with Owen's uncle. For all I knew, he could have fired me and covered it all up."

There was some sense to her statement. If Alexander found out his nephew was stealing money, Owen might not have been the only person in his crosshairs."

"What was Noelle's relationship with Clark?" I asked.

"They seemed friendly. I always thought he was nicer to her than he was to most people. I'm sure it's because he knew the family she married into had money. He's a suck-up when it comes to people with deep pockets."

"When you refused to talk to Clark, how did Noelle respond?"

"She was polite but adamant that Owen should have to come clean about what he'd done."

"Did Noelle suggest an alternative way to handle the situation —besides bringing the uncle into it?"

Annie tapped a finger to the table, thinking. "Noelle knew I was worried about my job. And though I didn't think Owen should get away with it, I didn't want to be the whistleblower. Noelle said she understood the predicament I was in. She suggested I keep going to work, act like it was business as usual, and to do what I could to stay under the radar."

As I assessed the story Annic had just told me, it made sense … in some ways.

In others, it didn't.

Why would Noelle, being as angry as Annie said she was about Owen's misdeeds, drop it just because Annie was frightened over keeping her job?

It seemed to me there was something else going on with Noelle.

But what?

The facts as I knew them:

1. Annie had seen blank company checks ripped out of the checkbook.
2. She'd seen Owen wearing an expensive watch, one he hadn't worn before.
3. The company books containing bank statements and so forth had disappeared.

Facts aside, it wasn't enough to go from speculation to accusation.

"I'm confused about Noelle's demeanor," I said. "If she was so upset over Owen's actions, why would she tell you to lie low?"

"It's a fair question. She was suggesting *I* take no action. She wanted me to leave it to her to sort out. She felt certain she could expose Owen without involving me in the process."

"What was her plan?"

"I don't know, and at the time, Noelle didn't know, either. She was going to take some time to think about it. She told me not to worry, even though it's all I've done ever since."

It was clear to me now why Noelle had discussed the matter with Zoey. She wanted to get a second opinion about what she should do.

"Do you know if Noelle ever confronted Owen or told anyone else what she knew?" I asked.

"I have no idea. When we discussed the matter, she said we shouldn't speak of it again, to protect me and my position, and we didn't."

Based on my interviews with those who knew Noelle, it seemed she'd gone to the grave leaving many of the reasons for her life's choices unexplained. I wished I could talk to her about the letter she'd written Gabe. I wish I knew whether she'd hired a private investigator to find the missing woman who'd fled the women's center. And then there was the matter of Owen. Had she questioned him about his potential thievery?

And if so, had she been murdered because of it?

Or was everything I knew so far unrelated to her murder?

Annie stood, slinging her purse over her shoulder. "I should be getting home. You have a dog waiting, and I have three cats."

"I know how hard it was for you to tell me what you just did, so thank you."

She nodded and left the office. As I started to gather my things, questions swirling around in my head, the office door opened.

Annie stepped back inside, folder in hand.

"There's one more thing," she said. "And I wasn't going to do this, but now … well, now it doesn't seem right if I don't."

"Go on."

"When I was talking about Owen before, you were confused about how I was so sure that he was the one stealing from the company."

"It's speculation, and maybe you're right, but I'm also still hung up on Noelle's anger over the situation. I've heard she was meek in nature, kind, and soft-spoken. So tell me, why was she so riled up? What else was going on in her life at the time? There must have been something making her more agitated than usual."

"All I can say is I'm doing this for Noelle, even though it worries me."

"You're doing *what* for her?"

"I've already told you I caught Owen taking a blank check, and I've told you about the watch."

"You have. Is there something else?"

"There is … What I haven't told you is, before Owen hid the books, I made a copy of the checks, to document which numbers were missing. I also made a copy of the financials, anything I couldn't get to add up. In my opinion, it proves it was him. The handwriting matches up, as you'll see, and I can confirm it's his. I'll give you these copies. All I ask is one thing in return—find the bastard who killed Noelle before anyone else gets murdered."

CHAPTER 21

I woke to find myself sitting on an outdoor balcony, glass of champagne in hand. I was dressed in the same black, floor-length nightgown I'd worn to bed, one I'd purchased from an antique store a week earlier. But the balcony I was on wasn't my own, nor was I alone. Sitting next to me was a woman in a pink dress, the shade of which matched her rose-colored cheeks.

The woman raised the champagne glass, toasting me. "Cheers."

We clinked glasses, though I wasn't sure what we were celebrating.

I looked over at her and said, "Where am I?"

"You know where you are, don't you? You've been here before."

I had, and at present, I was in a dream.

"I have been here before, Noelle. What are we celebrating tonight?"

"We're celebrating you."

"Why?"

"You're getting married soon, aren't you?"

"This summer," I said. "How did you know?"

"I like summer. Summer is warm and trusting, like being wrapped in a blanket in front of a roaring fire."

"I've never thought of it that way."

"Maybe it's time you start. What I don't like is winter."

"Why not?"

"Winter is like a trickster, full of lies."

"Why would you say such a thing?"

She tipped her head back, polishing off the rest of her champagne.

Then she stood.

"I should get us another bottle," she said. "Tonight is a special night. It's different because you're here. I don't know how long I have until I leave, or you leave. I say we make the most of our time together."

She walked toward the sliding glass door, and I turned, peering into a bedroom that contained a memory I'd tried hard to forget. As she reached for the door's handle, I glanced around the balcony, my eyes coming to rest on a bottle of champagne nestled inside a bucket of ice.

"Wait," I said.

Noelle glanced over her shoulder. "What is it?"

"There's no need to go inside." I pointed at my discovery. "There's another bottle of champagne right here. See?"

She turned around and leaned in, giving it a good look. "Oh, my. You're right. I'd forgotten it was there."

"Why is it outside, though—and not inside, with the others?"

"This one is special, a surprise I was saving until later."

"A surprise for whom?"

She stared into the darkness, a hollow look of emptiness on her face. "I suppose now it's a surprise for us. I'm sure he'll understand."

"Who will understand?"

She sat beside me again, putting her hand over mine. "Thank you for being with him in those final hours of his life. And thank you for what you're trying to do for me. I know how hard it must be for you to be here again. I feel it, the pain you carry, the guilt rushing through you."

"What do you know about my visit with your husband?"

"I know it's not your fault. He would have killed himself whether you were here that day or not. He was determined, and he'd made his decision. There was no talking him out of it."

"What about your daughter, left to live her life without a mother or a father now? How could he do that, knowing how she'd suffer?"

A breeze trickled by, blowing a mist of cool spring air.

Noelle breathed it in, smiling.

"I've seen what my husband would have become had he not chosen to take his own life," Noelle said. "Think of it like a sliding door, a glimpse down two paths, and what happens on each."

"What did you see?"

"Nothing good. Our daughter is receiving the best possible care now, and she is loved. She will suffer for a time, but she will go on to live a good life, a full life."

"How do you know?"

"I just do. I see things in a different way now, in ways that weren't possible when I was alive. It's as if a veil has been lifted."

I'd had many dreams I considered to be more than regular dreams in the past. None of them had been this clear, this easy to interpret and understand. There was something different happening now. I wondered why they'd changed.

"Why am I here, Noelle?" I asked.

"You chose to be here tonight, and I'm glad you are. Stay as long as you like. It's lonely, the days and nights all blending together until I'm not even certain what day it is anymore."

"Can't you leave?"

"Not yet, but soon." She paused, then added, "Tonight is different than the rest."

"How so?"

"Days repeat. I try to leave, and when I do, I find myself right back here again."

"Do you keep reliving what happened on the night you died?" I asked.

There was sorrow in her eyes as she said, "Death is a subject I don't care to talk about. Why speak of things so grim in this moment when we can speak of better times instead?"

Better times.

She wouldn't have more of those, not in this life.

Noelle grabbed her champagne glass, wiggling it at me. "Well, aren't you going to open it? I see no point in letting it go to waste."

I'd become so caught up in our conversation, I'd forgotten it was there.

I lifted the champagne out of the bucket, wiping the ice chips away as I glanced at the bottle. The label said Chateau Marmot, a champagne I had never heard of before. I wrapped a hand around the cork, twisting it until it came free, making a distinct popping sound as champagne fizzled out of the top.

"Looks like we lost a little bit," I said.

"Don't trouble yourself. There's still plenty for each of us."

I poured each of us a glass, and for a time we sat, sipping on champagne and enjoying echoes of sounds flowing through the coastal air. As much as I felt I could remain in this moment forever, I could not. I needed to make the most of it before I woke, as I doubted the opportunity would present itself again.

"I know you don't want to talk about what happened to you, but we should," I said.

She tipped her head to the side, blinking at me. "Can I ask you a question first?"

"Sure."

"You've had dreams like this before, haven't you?"

"I often do when I'm working a homicide investigation."

"Are they much the same?"

"They're not, though this one is far less confusing."

"In what way?"

I thought about the easiest way to explain it.

"This one is a lot clearer," I said.

"There's a reason for that, don't you think?"

I turned toward her. "I don't follow."

"You've never fully acknowledged these dreams."

"Yes, I have."

"What I mean to say is, you don't acknowledge they are anything more than your subconscious working overtime to understand things you're confused about."

I struggled to grasp her meaning.

"I've had dreams like these the majority of my life, starting when I was a child," I said. "I've always known they have a deeper meaning, but I don't always understand their interpretation."

"There are few in life you trust enough to share these dreams with, and when you do, you treat the dreams as if they're an extension of your subconscious. Maybe that's why they don't serve you in the way they could."

It felt as though she was trying to tell me something, but whatever it was, she wasn't coming right out and saying it.

"What is it you want me to know?" I asked.

"Have you ever considered you have a gift, something bigger than your physical self that you tap into when you need it the most?"

"I've never given it enough thought one way or the other."

"Of course you have. It's on your mind, even now. And still, you don't trust it enough to fully immerse yourself."

"I never said I don't trust it."

"You've never said you do. Why not?"

"If I admit these dreams are more than the fabric of my imagination, it would make me question myself," I said. "It would make me feel like it means I'm not normal."

"You're so much more than normal, and your gift … not only

should you trust it, but you should also lean into it, taking the wisdom and using it to assist you along the way. Only then will you see things with a lot more clarity."

I was starting to wonder if we were ever going to circle back to her murder.

"I'll give it some thought," I said.

"I'm glad."

"Can we talk about the night you died?"

"I will answer what I can. But first, more champagne."

I poured her another glass.

"Did you see the person who murdered you?" I asked.

"I saw everything."

"What can you tell me about it?"

"I can't. There are certain things you must realize for yourself."

"Why did you write Gabe a letter?"

"I wanted to move on from who he was, who I was, and I realized I couldn't until I forgave him."

"I've seen him. He seems like a changed man, but I don't know. I have another question. There was a woman who fled from the women's center. I know you wanted to hire a private investigator to find her. Did you?"

In the last couple of minutes, I'd noticed a shift in her appearance.

She was fading.

"It's been nice, sitting here, talking to you tonight," she said.

"Please don't go. I have so many questions you haven't answered yet."

"Look at me, Georgiana."

I did as she asked.

"What's in front of you is just as important as what's behind," she said. "Think about all we've discussed tonight, and know this, I've already told you everything you need to know."

CHAPTER 22

When I woke the next morning, my thoughts were still on the dream I'd had the night before and how it was unlike many of the others. What stuck in my mind was the comment Noelle had made about how she'd told me everything I needed to know, because I didn't believe she had.

Nothing she said pointed me to her killer.

Not yet.

I spent the morning with Luka, giving him the much-needed attention he lacked when I'd arrived home so late the night before. And while I was sure he would have preferred to go on a ride-along with me today, it didn't seem right to leave him in the car while I made the stops I needed to make.

As I slid my shoes on, he let out a soft whine, letting me know he wasn't thrilled I was leaving.

I bent down, giving him a quick scratch. "I'm sorry, buddy. I'll come home earlier today, okay? I promise."

He continued to brood, his eyes locked on me as I headed out the door.

I thought about who to see next, landing on Owen's uncle, Alexander Beaumont, and I headed to his home. Given he was well known in the area, finding his address had been easy. What wasn't easy was gaining an audience with him, as his sprawling estate was hidden behind a giant iron gate.

I approached it and looked around, my eyes coming to rest on an intercom system. I pressed the call button and waited.

A few seconds later, a male voice came through the intercom's speaker. "Can I help you?"

"Is Alexander home? I'd like to speak with him."

"Who are you?"

"My name is Georgiana Germaine."

"Do you have an appointment?"

"I don't, but I was hoping—"

"Alexander is a busy man, and he doesn't take walk-ins off the street."

He spoke to me like I was classless riffraff.

I let it slide, for now.

"I wasn't aware I needed an appointment," I said.

"What is the reason for your visit?"

"I'm a private investigator. I've been hired to investigate the death of Noelle Winters. Before she was murdered, she was an instructor at Royal Palms, the tennis club Alexander is an investor in."

"What does her death and the tennis club have to do with the purpose of your visit?"

If nothing else, at least he was thorough.

"I've been told Alexander is the biggest shareholder of the tennis club," I said. "And I have reason to believe Noelle's murder might be connected to the club in some way."

There was a long pause, and I wondered if he'd halted our communication.

"Hello?" I said. "Are you still there?"

"Just one moment, if you don't mind."

I did mind, but if waiting a moment allowed me to speak to Alexander, I could spare it.

One minute went by, and then two, and then …

"Mr. Beaumont doesn't have time to speak with you today, Miss Germaine," he said. "Like I said, he's a busy man."

"And I'm a busy woman. Is there any chance he'd reconsider? I'll be brief."

"Have a nice day, Miss Germaine. Goodbye."

I considered my next move.

"I'll ask you to leave now," he said.

"Did you even tell Alexander who I am and why I'm here?"

"I saw no reason to disturb him."

"So, no, then. Okay, fine. I'll wait here until a few minutes in his schedule free up. I imagine he has to leave the house at some point, right? I'll be right here when he does."

"You cannot loiter at the front gate."

"I can, and I will."

"If you're not going to respect my decision, I'm sorry to say I'll have to call the police."

"Go ahead—they're friends of mine. I'm sure they'd like to hear what I have to say. Here I was thinking it might be best to share the private information I've come across with Alexander *before* I took it to the police, as it will interest him. But now …"

He huffed an impatient, "I'll tell him you're here, but if he doesn't wish to see you, I'll expect you to leave."

"Fine."

A couple of minutes later, the gate opened, and I made my way to the front of the house. I was met by a tall, shrewd-looking man with a large, narrow nose and beady eyes. He was standing in front of the towering double doors at the home's entrance, his arms crossed.

"You must be Intercom Guy," I said.

"What makes you think I'm not Alexander?"

"A few things."

He was well dressed, but he didn't have the right air about him.

He struck me as a person who was second in command, not first.

I didn't elaborate, instead asking, "What's your name?"

"Max Sterling."

"It's nice to meet you."

I waited for him to return the sentiment.

He did not.

"You let me in, Max," I said. "Now what?"

"I've let Mr. Beaumont know you're here, and against my better judgment, he's eager to speak with you. Come with me."

I followed him inside to a sitting room the size of a modest house. Once there, he pointed at a black velvet chair and said, "Sit here, and Mr. Beaumont will be with you in a moment."

"When you say *in a moment*, is it an actual moment or more like the wait I just had outside when you said the same thing?"

Max didn't find my attempt at humor amusing, and he turned, leaving the room without offering a response. Unable to resist the urge, I cupped a hand to the side of my mouth, saying, "By the way, your tie is crooked."

If the man didn't despise me before, he did now.

Max had just turned the corner when another man walked in. He was in his early eighties, I guessed, and bald, though it didn't take away from his distinguished style and good looks. From his polished shoes to the blue pocket square and black tailored suit, everything about him was impeccable.

He approached and said, "Miss Germaine, is it?"

I nodded, and he stuck out a hand, which I accepted.

"Alexander Beaumont, nice to meet you." He took a seat across from me. "I hear you're on the Noelle Winters case. How's it going, if you don't mind me asking?"

"I've had a bit of a slow start, but I'm gathering together a shortlist of suspects, and it's looking a lot more promising."

"Good to know. What is it you've come to see me about?"

"I was told you're the biggest investor of the tennis club."

"Yes, tennis was my late wife's passion."

"I'm sorry to hear she's passed on."

"She's been gone for over three years now. To me, it still feels like yesterday when I held her hand, said goodbye. You can have all the money in the world, but money means nothing when you can't save the person you love. I tried, I sure tried. No matter. She's gone now. Did you know Noelle and my wife were good friends?"

"I did not."

"They often played tennis together. My wife found Noelle to be a formidable opponent."

"I hear Noelle was a talented player in her younger years."

"Talented, and then some. What is your interest in my investment in the club?"

"Your nephew, Owen. He works there, doesn't he?"

"He does."

"I hear he was transferred to the accounting department in the last year."

Alexander leaned over, ringing a miniature bell sitting on a gold plate on the side table. A young woman came in, looking his way as she said, "What can I get for you, Sir?"

"Oolong tea, please, Marianne." He then turned toward me. "Would you care for anything to drink, Miss Germaine?"

"I'm fine, thank you."

Marianne left the room, and he said, "Now, where were we?"

"I'd just asked about Owen being transferred to the accounting department."

"Oh, yes. I'll admit I had a hand in him obtaining the position. He liked his previous position a whole lot more, but it was useless, a job anyone could have done. I didn't assist with his college tuition to have him sucking up to clientele all day."

"Have you spoken to him since he took over the accounting department?"

"I wouldn't call it a 'department,' given he manages the books himself."

"Are you saying no one else works with him?"

"Not to my knowledge, no. The club is a decent size but not substantial enough to require a team, not when Owen's so capable."

It seemed Alexander was unaware Annie had been hired to assist Owen.

"Has Clark talked to you about how Owen's doing in his new position?" I asked.

"We've spoken by phone a couple of times. Everything seems to be going well. I've heard nothing to the contrary. Why do you ask?"

"I'm curious about his bookkeeping. Does anyone ever look over the books to make sure everything is in order?"

"Why wouldn't it be?"

I gave the question some thought, trying to think of the right way to say what needed to be said. Whenever possible, I told the truth, but in this instance, I had Annie to consider. I needed to find a way to keep her name out of it, and if lying protected her, then it was a lie I would tell.

"Miss Germaine, can I be straight with you?" he asked.

"Of course."

"I'm a man who prefers frankness more than anything," he said. "Whatever it is you've come to say, I do wish you'd come right out and say it so we can both get on with our day."

He may have preferred frankness, but once I gave him the information I had on Owen, I wondered if he'd feel the same way.

I was about to find out.

CHAPTER 23

"I have reason to believe your nephew has been stealing money from the tennis club, writing checks to himself and cashing them, and no doubt altering the financials to cover his tracks," I said.

We locked eyes for a time, and I waited for him to speak.

"That's a big accusation," he said. "How did you come by it?"

"Before Noelle died, she suspected Owen was stealing company money. I don't know how she figured it out, but she told a friend her suspicions, someone unrelated to the club in any way. Not long after, she was murdered."

"This *friend* she confided in, will you give me her name?"

"It's in her best interest if I do not."

He grinned. "I don't blame you. I'd do the same. In the spirit of frankness, this wouldn't be the first time Owen has been accused of thievery. He was visiting my home over the summer some years ago, and the maid caught him trying to steal one of my watches."

High-end watches seemed to be Owen's kryptonite.

"Did he confess?" I asked.

"After much deliberation, yes."

"Would it surprise you to hear he's been wearing an expensive Cartier watch?"

"It would not. I gave it to him when he began his new position. As to the allegation you've brought against him, I assume you wouldn't have done so unless you had proof."

It was time for the big lie.

I reached into my handbag, pulling out a copy of the documents Annie had given to me.

"Noelle wanted to prove her suspicions about Owen were accurate, so she snuck into his office when he wasn't there, and she copied a few things," I said.

It was, in my opinion, the perfect lie.

Noelle wasn't alive to corroborate the story, and I hoped it seemed feasible enough to keep Annie in the clear.

I handed over the copies, and he leaned back, flipping through one page after the other. When he finished, he tossed the pages to the floor, and they scattered at our feet. He shouted a few expletives and then said, "I must apologize. It's not often I speak in such a way. I thought Owen had learned his lesson some time ago. It appears he has not."

"It's all right," I said. "I'd like to apologize myself. It doesn't feel good to come here and tell you what I just did."

"You did the right thing, the honest thing."

The *mostly* honest thing.

"I am grateful to you," he added. "Who knows how long this would have gone on, how much damage he's already done, or the lengths I'll have to go to in order to clean up his mess."

"What will you do?"

"Whatever is necessary. I feel I must ask—why come to me and not go to Clark or to Owen himself?"

"Given your family's reputation, I thought this situation warranted a level of discretion."

"I appreciate it, and you're correct. There is a right way to handle these matters and a wrong way."

Marianne returned to the room with a tray. On it was a china tea set. She set it on the side table, pouring him a cup. Before she handed it over to him, she dropped in two sugar cubes and a dollop of honey, giving it a quick stir. She passed it off, and he took a sip, thanking her.

For a man with considerable wealth, in the short time I'd spent with him, I found him to be an almost-perfect gentleman. I hoped he'd remain that way when I said what I was about to say.

"As you know, I'm investigating Noelle's murder," I said. "I have to look at all suspects, anyone who had a reason to kill her."

"I believe I know the direction you're going in on this subject, but please, continue."

"Owen is my main suspect."

"I assumed as much."

"I'm not sure whether Noelle confronted him with the information she'd found before she died," I said. "If she did, and it turns out he had anything to do with her murder, I won't have a choice as far as how it will need to be handled."

"I believe you're saying you won't be able to protect my family's reputation in the way you're doing now."

I nodded. "I hope he's innocent, for your sake. I won't know until I do a little more digging."

"I understand. Is there anything else?"

"That's all."

"Since you've been so candid with me, allow me to do the same before you leave. Noelle requested an audience with me before she died."

"When?"

"As it turns out, the day before she was murdered."

"Did you meet with her?"

"I did not. She canceled, saying she was running behind on an engagement party she was planning. She asked to speak with me the following week."

"Did Noelle say why she wanted to see you?"

"She did not, though she did say she needed my advice."

Why would she need his advice about Owen?

Why not just tell Alexander what his nephew was doing and let him sort it out for himself?

I stood, thanking him for his time.

As we walked together toward the front of the house, he lifted a finger, turning in my direction as he said, "There's something I'd like you to do for me, if it's not too much to ask, of course."

"Name it."

"Can I trouble you to stop by Royal Palms this morning? I'd like you to tell Clark what you just told me."

"I can. I just figured you'd want to tell him yourself."

"I have a full schedule for the rest of the day, and I rather think it would be best presented by you, someone who can remain calm, as I would not be. Had Clark been running a tighter ship, I don't believe I'd be in the predicament I'm in now. That's not to say I blame him for my nephew's actions. I do not. If Noelle suspected Owen, a woman who wasn't even part of management, Clark should have too."

I resisted the urge to bring up a valid point. I was certain Clark's main agenda was keeping Alexander happy. Micromanaging his nephew would have achieved the opposite.

"It makes sense," I said.

"Wonderful. I'll have a message sent to him, letting him know you'll be stopping by. Please tell him that what the two of you discuss isn't to be talked about with anyone until he receives further instructions from me. If he wants to keep his job, he'll keep this quiet. As to my nephew, I'll speak to him personally."

CHAPTER 24

My second visit to Royal Palms was far more welcoming than the first, and I arrived to find Clark ready and waiting, standing by the front door as if anticipating my arrival. As I approached, he held the door open for me. "Miss Germaine, it's good to see you."

Good to see me?

I doubted he meant it, but I appreciated his change in tone, and I had to admit, I enjoyed Clark 2.0 way more than the 1.0 version.

"Has Alexander been in contact with you?" I asked.

"I suppose … in his way."

"What's his way?"

"He often communicates with me through Max."

"We met this morning. He's an interesting guy."

Clark looked around as if concerned about who was in our immediate vicinity. For the moment, the two of us were alone.

Leaning toward me, he said, "I was thinking we might take a walk. There's a park across the street. What do you say we have our conversation there?"

"Why not talk in your office? Is there any reason why we can't?"

He lowered his voice and said, "The architect did an excellent job designing the club, although they skimped on the budget when it came to soundproofing. Let's just say the walls aren't as thick as I would like. And since I haven't been made fully aware of the reason for your visit, I wouldn't want to take the chance that someone might overhear our conversation."

Given it was a sunny day, and almost sixty degrees outside, a chat in the park didn't seem like a bad idea.

"What do you know of our meeting?" I asked.

"Not much. I've been told Alexander sent you to discuss something with me. Whatever it is, Max made it sound like it's a big deal."

I nodded, and we started walking toward the park, engaging in small talk along the way.

"How long have you been managing the tennis club?" I asked.

"Oh, let's see … it's been about twelve years now."

"Do you like your job?"

"I love it."

"Do you have a tennis background?"

"Sure do. When I was in my early twenties, there was a time when I thought I had a shot at going pro."

"What happened?" I asked.

"I was in a car accident, hit by a drunk driver. Several bones were broken, including one of my arms. The healing process took a lot longer than expected. After several months, I was cleared to play again, and I couldn't wait. There was just one problem. Even though I thought my injuries were behind me, I struggled to get back into the game, and I never played the same way again."

"It must have been hard to give up on your dream."

"Harder than you can imagine. Prior to the accident, tennis was my entire life. I lived and breathed it, often at the expense of everything and everyone else. I was devastated."

"Looking at you now, you seem to have found a way to get past it."

"My biggest tragedy turned into my biggest blessing when I met my wife, Heidi. I was in a dark place when we first met, and she pulled me out of it."

"Are the two of you still married?"

"We are. What about you? Are you married?"

"Not yet. I'm engaged."

"When's the wedding?"

"August, in New York."

As the small talk simmered down, I shifted gears.

"During my first visit, you didn't treat me the way you are now," I said. "Part of me thinks Alexander's influence is the reason for the sudden change of heart. I also think there's more to it. Mind sharing?"

He cleared his throat. "I'd like to apologize for my brusqueness in tone when we first met. I wasn't having a good day. Ever since Noelle died, there's been a lot of gossip going around the club, employees speculating about what happened to her and why. It's been … well, in a word, exhausting."

"Your employees are no different than everyone else in this town. People find great discomfort in the unknown, and often-times, they create their own narrative, even though none of us knows what happened to Noelle, or why, yet."

He nodded, reaching into his pocket and pulling out a stick of gum. "Want some?"

"No, thanks. I didn't know they still made Bubble Magic."

"I didn't either until a toy store opened in the outlet center in San Luis Obispo. They carry all kinds of things from past generations."

He unwrapped the stick of gum and popped it in his mouth. "It came to my attention that some of my staff have been speaking to our members about Noelle's death. Right before you arrived, I called a meeting. I made it clear I didn't want anyone spreading false information about Noelle's murder, not with their fellow staff and not with our members. It's like you said, no one knows what happened, and there's no point in making assumptions."

His reasoning made sense.

We arrived at the park, taking a seat at one of the picnic tables. He wasted no time getting right to the point of our meeting.

"How do you know Alexander?" he asked.

"I didn't know him, not until today."

"I'm shocked he granted you an audience. He turns most people away, including me. I've never been allowed to step foot inside his house."

"I wasn't sure he'd agree to meet with me. At first. Max turned me away, but I didn't leave. It took a lot of convincing before he told Alexander I was there."

"Why do you think Alexander agreed to see you?"

"His late wife was friends with Noelle."

"Ahh, yes, I remember. His wife was a sweet woman. It was a shame she died."

"How did she die? I didn't dare ask."

"It was a bit unusual. She overdosed on her prescription medication."

"Why is that unusual?" I asked.

"She always seemed so well put together, not like someone who would make a mistake with their medication. But what do I know?"

Maybe it was a bit strange.

I put the thought to the side for now.

"When I spoke to Alexander, he didn't seem to know you'd hired Annie," I said.

Clark's face went pale. "You didn't mention her to him, did you?"

"I did not, but I'm thinking you should. If he finds out you kept it from him, you'll be a lot worse off than if you just level with the guy."

"I've kept it from him for far too long. I'm not sure how to fix it now."

He was right.

Given she'd worked there for months, he'd put himself in a predicament.

I thought on it a moment and came up with an idea.

"Maybe you don't have to mention how long Annie has worked at the club. Why not slide her into Owen's position without mentioning how long she's worked there?"

He furrowed his brow, confused. "Why would Annie take over Owen's position? I'll admit, he's somewhat of a dimwit. If it wasn't for Alexander, I would never have moved him to accounting. He was great in client relations. Everyone loved him. There's no way Alexander would allow me to change Owen's position."

"Oh, there's where you're wrong."

"What do you know that I don't?"

The time had come to share the reason for my visit.

"Owen has been stealing money, writing checks to himself and cashing them," I said.

Clark looked at me, his expression like I'd just made a joke. When he realized I wasn't joking at all, he ran a hand along his jaw, his body language indicating he had no knowledge of Owen's misdeeds.

"How can you be certain?" he asked.

I initiated my *white lie* button once again, saying, "Noelle suspected Owen was embezzling money from the club. And before you ask, I don't know how she first came to suspect him. All I know is, she made copies of some of the company's files in his office. Here, let me show you."

I handed him a copy of the copy of the files Annie had given me, then I crossed my arms, resting them on the table as he went through them.

Once he finished, he said, "How could this happen without me knowing about it? And if Noelle suspected him, why didn't she come to me?"

I could think of a solid reason why he hadn't noticed.

In his quest to keep Alexander happy, Clark left Owen unchecked.

"Did Alexander tell you what I'm supposed to do with this information?" he asked.

"He wants you to keep it to yourself, for now. He said something about staying quiet if you want to keep your job."

"Got it."

"As I was leaving his house, he said he would deal with Owen."

"What am I supposed to do with him until then?"

"Nothing."

"Do you know how hard it's going to be to act like I don't know this information?"

"Maybe do your best to avoid interacting with Owen—as much as you can, at least—until Alexander gets in touch with him."

"How long do you think Alexander will wait before talking to Owen?"

"I can't say, though after meeting the man, I'm sure he'll want to deal with all this right away."

"What if more money goes missing in the meantime?"

Having delivered Alexander's message, I had a lot of stops to make.

I stood, offering Clark a parting word of advice.

"What's important right now is that you don't let on that you know what's happening," I said. "I have no doubt Alexander will deal with it in his own way and in his own time, and I suggest you let him do just that."

CHAPTER 25

"I need to ask you a strange question," I said.

I was sipping on a latte in Whitlock's SUV, outside 2 Little Figs coffee shop.

"In my opinion, there are no strange questions," Whitlock said. "What's up?"

"Dominic and Noelle had a balcony off the side of their bedroom."

"Yes, I remember."

"When you searched the house, did you find anything there, aside from a couple of chairs?"

Whitlock gave the question some thought. "As a matter of fact, we did. Why do you ask?"

"No reason."

Whitlock didn't seem to be buying it. He tipped his head to the side, looking at me like he suspected I was withholding something from him. I thought back to the dream I'd had, about what Noelle had said about me leaning into my dreams, realizing they are a gift, and trusting them more.

"I … ahh, I've talked to you about some of the dreams I've had in the past," I said. "I don't know why I still get nervous about mentioning new ones. I guess I still feel a bit weird about them as a whole."

He reached for his coffee and turned toward me. "Can I share something with you?"

"Sure."

"When your father was alive, we got to talking one night when we were doing a stakeout. He told me you woke up in the middle of the night after having a bad dream. He heard you crying, and he went to your room. Do you remember?"

"I don't. What was the dream about?"

"You told him you dreamed about a man drowning a woman in a pool. You remembered she had blond hair and wore a red dress. You also described a ring the man was wearing. It was silver and had a skull on it."

"Wow, I can't believe I don't remember."

"The next day, we received a call about a homicide. When we got to the house, we found a woman floating in the pool. Blond hair, red dress."

"And the man with the ring?"

"It took a few months, but then we got a good lead on a suspect. We went to the guy's house to bring him in for question-ing. First thing we noticed was the ring he was wearing—silver with a skull."

I was in shock.

"I wonder why my father never mentioned that to me," I said.

"You were so young at the time. I think your father thought it best not to burden you with the weight of your clairvoyant moment. He didn't even tell your mother."

"What age was I at the time?"

"You couldn't have been any older than six."

Six years old.

It was a lot to take in.

My earliest memory of having these kinds of dreams was when I was ten. At the time, I didn't talk to anyone about it. I feared no one would believe me. I also worried I'd be made fun of, so I stuck to the people I trusted—my parents.

"What did you find on the balcony?" I asked.

He glanced at me, a huge grin on his face as he said, "You tell me, kiddo."

"Champagne on ice. I think Noelle put it outside during the engagement party or just prior to it. My guess is she'd intended on sharing it with Dominic later that night. She said it was a special bottle, not like the others."

"Anything else about the dream? That is, if you feel like talking about it."

"Nothing that adds to our investigation right now. What about you? Do you have anything new to share?"

"All roads have led to dead ends, as far as we're concerned."

"Foley was supposed to talk to Donnelly, the chief of police in Santa Maria, about the women who came forward about their abuse. Has he met with him yet?"

"Donnelly's on vacation. He'll be back in a few days. Say, what was your take on Gabe Romero?"

"Before I met him in person, I thought he'd be our prime suspect," I said.

"And now?"

"Unless he's mastered the art of putting on a good façade, I don't think he's involved. Most people don't change. They are who they are. But Gabe, he's … well, not like I expected him to be."

"I agree. Anyone else you're looking at?"

"Owen Beaumont," I said. "He's the nephew of the multimillionaire Alexander Beaumont. He works at Royal Palms, the tennis club. Last year, he was promoted to head of the accounting department. It seems he's been giving himself a five-finger discount with some of the club's money."

"Stealing from the club, eh? How do you know?"

I finished my mocha, setting the cup in the holder. "Noelle

used to teach tennis lessons at the club once a week. She became friends with one of their employees, Annie Jackson, who'd been hired to assist Owen. Before I go any further, I should mention Annie is afraid Noelle may have been murdered because Annie told her about the missing money. If it is related, and I'm not sure if it is yet, she's worried someone will come after her next. I've had to tell a few lies to protect her. So far, it seems to be working."

"Gotcha."

"Right after Annie was hired, she started to suspect Owen was skimming off the top. After catching him tearing a blank check out of the company checkbook, she told Noelle what she thought was going on."

"Did Noelle do something about it … or?"

"She told Zoey over lunch one day. My guess is she was trying to figure out how best to handle the situation. What I don't know is whether she confronted Owen about it or not."

"Have you asked him?"

"I haven't. I decided to go a different route. This morning, I paid a visit to Alexander after learning he has a vested interest in the club. He also was responsible for Owen getting the accounting position."

"What did he have to say?"

"When I told him what his nephew has been up to, and I showed him proof of it, he acted surprised. Well, not surprised … maybe more disappointed than anything."

"What made you decide to go to him first?"

"Given his family is well known, I wanted to give him the opportunity to handle it in a discreet manor. I also wanted to gauge his reaction to the news, face to face. He alleges he had no idea Owen had been taking money from the club."

"Do you believe him?"

"I want to believe him, but I can't rule him out as a suspect. Not yet."

Whitlock raised a brow. "A suspect? What are you thinking?"

"It's nothing more than a theory right now. Alexander told me Noelle tried to speak with him, but she couldn't before she died. What if he's lying? What if she did speak to him and told him what she knew? Dominic and Noelle were on the wealthy side too. It's easy to believe the two families mingled in the same circles. Alexander even admitted Noelle and his late wife were friends."

"Ahh, so your theory is Noelle went to see Alexander, and to protect the family, he … what, killed her?"

"I don't see him getting his hands dirty."

"He hired someone to do it for him, then."

"Like I said, it's just a theory. My other theory is Noelle may have confronted Owen herself, but the more thought I've given it, the more I believe she wouldn't have gone to him."

"Why not?"

"If she told Owen what she knew, it's possible he would have figured out Noelle learned the information through Annie, since they were friends."

"Can't the same be said for Alexander?"

"Get this, to my knowledge, Alexander doesn't know Annie was hired to assist Owen with his job."

"How do you know?"

"He made no mention of her during our visit. And when I questioned Clark, the club manager about it today, he admitted he hasn't told him about her."

"Why not?"

"Given Alexander handpicked his nephew for the position when it became available, it may anger him to learn Clark hired him an accounting assistant because his nephew isn't the greatest at his job."

"Makes sense." Whitlock's attention shifted from me to a butterfly fluttering across the windshield. "Did you know most adult butterflies live less than a few weeks?"

"I did not."

"At least it's longer than the life of a mayfly. Their life span as adults is a single day."

"Glad I'm not a mayfly."

"You and me both. What's on the agenda for the rest of your day?"

"I thought I'd head over to the women's center and talk to Barbara Adams. She runs the place. I want to know more about one of the women who visited the clinic and then disappeared. Noelle thought about hiring a private detective to find her."

"Any idea why?"

"When she entered the clinic, she had a lot of bruising, and it was obvious she'd been beaten. After seeing the doctor, the woman fled. She hasn't been seen since."

"Huh, makes sense Noelle would want to hire someone to find her. Wonder if they ever did."

I grabbed my coffee cup, opened the door, and hopped out, saying, "If I find anything out, I'll let you know. Thanks for the coffee."

CHAPTER 26

The Ophelia Albrecht Women's Center was a bright-white, two-story building. With its large wraparound porch and Grecian columns, it reminded me of the house in *Gone with the Wind*. I stepped inside, quick to notice the elegant, winding staircase and the wall next to it, which boasted a floor-to-ceiling mural of a lotus flower. Known for their ability to rise from the mud without so much as a blemish, lotus flowers symbolized strength, resilience, and rebirth—the perfect choice for a women's center.

After I checked in with one of the security guards, I was given directions to Barbara's office. As I made my way there, I passed by a woman wearing a pink track suit. She glanced at me for a quick second and then looked away, grabbing her shirt sleeve and yanking it down as if trying to hide the cuts I'd just seen. In that moment, I felt a range of emotions—gratitude for places like this one mixed with a heaping feeling of sadness. I couldn't imagine what these women were going through and how brave they were to seek help.

I entered Barbara's office, and she smiled, looking up at me and saying, "Georgiana Germaine, it's nice to meet you. I was wondering when you'd stop by."

She was younger than I expected, forty-ish, and dressed in a black, rayon pantsuit. Her long, dark hair was pulled into a neat side bun.

"I wasn't aware you'd heard about me," I said.

"I looked you up after having a chat with Noelle's mother yesterday."

"How's Joanie doing?"

"She's been better. Do me a favor and close the door. I'm guessing the conversation we're about to have would be best had in private."

I closed the door, and she gestured at a chair.

I sat down.

"How are things going with your investigation?" she asked.

"A little slow, but I'm gaining momentum."

"I'm glad to hear it. It's been hard, being at work these past several days. It's difficult to stay strong, when all I want to do is to break down and cry. But I have no choice, I must be strong for the women at the center. They deserve it."

"Were you and Noelle close?"

"I'd like to think so. I was hired to manage the center right before it opened, and I've been here ever since."

"I heard Dominic went to great lengths to keep Noelle's name discreet, given the nature of the center and the services it provides."

"Dominic was protective of all of us, always thinking of ways to keep us, and the women who come here, safe. We give our first names to the women, but not our last, and we don't talk to the ladies about our personal lives … not often, anyway. Sometimes it's easier said than done."

"I bet."

"We form bonds with some of the women while they're here. It's easy to do."

I crossed one leg over the other. "Have you had many problems with any of the abusers showing up here, looking for their wives or girlfriends? I assume some of them know this is where they might go when they become brave enough to leave."

"We've had a few run-ins over the years, but I've got the police on speed dial, and the security here is excellent. And our two security guards are intimidating—in size as well as demeanor. Dominic and Noelle did a great job of creating a center where women feel protected from the outside world while they seek treatment and make plans to better their lives."

"Would you say most women who come here leave their abusers for good?"

Barbara shook her head, looking shocked at my question. "I'd say it's the opposite. About half of the women who return to their former relationships are abused again within six months. I choose to focus on the success stories—the women who are able to move forward. We help them all the best we can, which is all we can do. At the end of the day, it's their life and their decision."

"What will happen to the center now that Dominic and Noelle are dead?"

Barbara sighed, her expression one of concern. "I was just talking about this subject with Noelle's mother. She'd like the center to remain open and for us to continue to honor what Noelle started. But she has no idea what it takes to run this place, let alone to keep it funded enough to help these ladies. I'm nervous about it, to be honest. It takes a lot of money to run the center, but for now, we'll remain open as long as we can."

She paused, looking out the window at the woman in the pink track suit who was now strolling through the garden. Then she turned back to me, saying, "Now, what can I do for you?"

"In the weeks prior to Noelle's death, did anything happen with any of the women, anything out of the ordinary? Did Noelle act any different than usual?"

She gave my questions some thought. "Nothing out of the ordinary occurred at the center, no. As to your question about Noelle, no. She wasn't her usual, chipper self."

"Any idea why?"

"I always thought Noelle did a good job of keeping boundaries between herself and the women who come here—getting close, but not *too* close. About a month ago, that all changed."

"What happened?"

"A woman showed up one night in bad shape. She'd been beaten far worse than most I've seen, and I've seen a lot."

"Is this the same woman who left this place and then went missing?"

Barbara raised a brow. "Ah, I see you've heard of Dawn Salisbury."

"Noelle's mother told me about her. She said Noelle wanted to hire a private investigator to find Dawn. When she asked her mother for advice, Joanie told her to leave it alone."

"Sounds like something Joanie would say. She may have suggested Noelle do nothing, but between us, she did."

I leaned forward. "Are you saying Noelle hired a private investigator?"

"She sure did."

"And?"

"He couldn't find Dawn. It's like she just vanished. When the police stopped by her place, she wasn't there. Her apartment hadn't been packed up, and her car was still in the garage."

"Did anyone see Dawn after she left the center?"

"According to the private investigator, no. This center was the last place she was seen."

It was odd.

Even odder were the lengths to which Noelle had gone to find the woman, something she hadn't done with others in the past.

What was different about Dawn?

Was she the key to finding Noelle's murderer?

"When Dawn showed up here, what did she say about all her injuries?" I asked.

"She wouldn't admit to being abused, even though it was clear she had been. Noelle did everything she could to get Dawn to talk, but she wouldn't. Not to us, not to the police."

"Why do you think Noelle went out of her way to find Dawn? I'm assuming she didn't do the same for any of the other women."

Another glance out the window and then, "No, she didn't, and I've asked myself the same question many times. The situation with Dawn was unusual."

"In what way?"

"When she first got here, Noelle thought she'd seen her somewhere before."

"Even if that's true, it still doesn't explain why she'd hire someone to find her."

"I agree, and I should add, part of me suspected there was more to it—something Noelle wasn't telling me."

It made me wonder whether Noelle *knew* where she'd seen Dawn before, and for whatever reason, hadn't admitted it.

"What made you feel Noelle was keeping something from you?" I asked.

"Most of the time, when Noelle tried to get one of the women to speak their truth, admit who was hurting them, she did so in a calm, nonaggressive way. With Dawn, she pushed a lot harder."

"Do you think it was because of how badly she'd been beaten?"

"Maybe, I don't know."

"The private investigator she hired should have given Noelle a file folder with his findings, even if he didn't locate Dawn. You wouldn't happen to have it or know where it is, would you?"

She interlaced her fingers over the top of her desk, giving the question some thought. "I don't know anything about a file he may have given her, but since you're here, let's go check Noelle's office."

We stood and walked across the hall.

Barbara unlocked the door, and we stepped inside. She closed her eyes, breathing in a lungful of air. "I haven't been in here since … you know, prior to Noelle's death. I still remember the last time I was in here, talking to her. It was the day of the murder. She stopped by to grab something she needed for Zoey's engagement party."

"When people die, I always find rooms like these to be like time capsules. You almost don't want to touch or change anything."

"We won't, not right now. As far as I'm concerned, this is still her office."

Barbara walked to the other side of the desk, pulled the top drawer open, and riffled through it, taking things out and setting them on the desk. On her fifth try, she said, "Hey, I think I found something."

She pulled out a file folder out and opened it, nodding.

Sure enough, it was a summary of the investigation.

"Here you are," she said, handing it over. "I hope this helps."

CHAPTER 27

I was standing in the office kitchen, talking to Simone and Hunter about where we were in Noelle's murder investigation.

"If any of the guests who were still there at the end of Zoey's engagement party are involved in Noelle's murder, I can't find any proof of it," Simone said. "No one I've talked to seemed suspicious to me, at least."

"Have you spoken to everyone?" I asked.

"Yep, and they all seemed fine to talk to me about what they remembered from that night."

"Were there any new details, anything someone remembered that we didn't know before?"

"None whatsoever."

It wasn't what I was hoping to hear.

"Did you take a look at the photos I gave you?" I asked.

"Not only did I look at them, I used a magnifying glass to see if there were any details that would help us. I came up with nothing."

"What about Lenore?" I asked. "How did your conversation with her go?"

"I spoke to her last night. She was a lot less chatty than I expected. She answered my questions but said little beyond that. For someone who didn't know Dominic well, she's sure upset about his death."

Of course she was upset.

Her rags-to-riches dreams had just been dashed.

"I was hoping we'd get somewhere with the few guests who remained until the lights went out and all hell broke loose," I said. "Maybe we need to cast a wider net, check with the guests who were there earlier in the evening, see where they went after the party and if they have alibis for the time of Noelle's murder."

"I can do that. Might take a while."

"It's all right. I'm thinking the divide-and-conquer approach might be the best way of catching this guy."

"What about you?" Hunter asked. "What's happened since we last met?"

I filled them in on the places I'd been, the people I'd seen, and the ones I suspected the most.

"Sounds like your main suspects are tied to the tennis club in some way," Hunter said. "Do you want me to get background information on any of them?"

"Alexander Beaumont strikes me as a person who would pay to keep things quiet to protect his family," I said. "Not that I fault him for it. The more money a person makes, the more everything needs to be safeguarded. Go ahead, shake some trees, and let's see what falls out."

"It feels like we're being pulled in different directions with this case," Simone said. "I can't make sense of it, or why Noelle was murdered."

"I agree—we're missing something, a key point. Once I figure out what it is, I'm sure all our questions will be answered. We just have to keep pushing."

"Is there anything else we can do to help you?" Simone asked.

"Not right now. I think I'm going to head home earlier than

usual and soak in the hot tub while I go over the file Barbara gave me. Why don't we regroup in the morning?"

"Sounds great," Hunter said.

She hopped off the kitchen counter, grabbing her hoodie and slipping it on.

"You two go on ahead," I said. "I'll be right behind you."

As I watched them walk out the door, I began thinking about the file I needed to go through. Then I thought about the notes I'd taken since the case started. It was possible going over them one more time would prove useful. I grabbed them out of my desk drawer and slipped them into my handbag next to the file folder.

My cell phone rang, and I answered it. "I was just going to call you."

"I wanted to check in," Zoey said. "Are you any closer to finding out what happened to Noelle?"

"I'd say so. I have a few good leads."

I heard what sounded like clapping on the other end of the line, and then she said, "I'm glad to hear it."

"How are things with Lucas? Did the two of you have a good talk?"

"We had a great talk. He apologized for leaving, and I apologized for … well, everything. We're back together, though I'm not sure we were ever apart. The wedding is still *off* for now. We've decided to wait until I'm in a better place."

"I'm glad to hear it. You sound a lot better than you did the last time we talked."

"Hiring you has helped put me at ease. I know you're going to solve this case. I feel it in my gut."

I did too.

And my gut was telling me I was a lot closer to solving it than it may have seemed.

"I was going to call you this evening to fill you in, but also, I have a question for you," I said. "Did Noelle ever mention a woman who came to the center named Dawn Salisbury?"

"The woman who went missing? Yeah, she told me about her. Why do you ask?"

"Noelle hired a private investigator to find Dawn, but he couldn't. It just seems strange to me that Noelle tempered her relationships with most of the women, but then Dawn came along, and Noelle hired someone to search for her."

"Yeah, when you put it that way, I guess it is strange."

"Noelle thought she'd seen the woman somewhere before, but she wasn't sure where."

"I know where."

"What do you mean?"

"She saw her before in the parking lot at the tennis club, talking to someone. No, wait … *arguing* with someone."

"Arguing with whom?"

"Umm, I don't know. She didn't give me a name."

"I find it suspicious that the same woman who came to the center and then went missing just so happens to have been in an argument with someone at the same place Noelle taught tennis lessons."

"I'm guessing you're thinking it's not a coincidence."

It wasn't one.

Of that, I was certain.

CHAPTER 28

I locked the office door and walked to my car, thinking about the comment I'd made to Simone and Hunter about Alexander Beaumont being the kind of person who would go to great lengths to protect his family. It made me wonder … maybe stealing from the tennis club wasn't the only dirty deed in Owen's life. Maybe he had a habit of abusing women—a habit that had been covered up and cleaned up whenever it reared its ugly head.

Was murder part of the clean-up process?

Would Alexander go that far to help his nephew?

Or was I going about it all wrong, perhaps blaming the wrong Beaumont?

While Alexander was getting up there in age, he was fit, which wasn't to say he'd take it upon himself to deal with Noelle. The notion seemed far-fetched. If he had murdered her, he would have had to find a way to get into Noelle's house during the party without being seen. Then he'd have to get upstairs, again without being seen. Once there, he would have had to wait for the opportune time to strike. Then leave—without being seen.

I couldn't envision it at all.

The more likely story—*if* Noelle's murder was Alexander's

doing—was that he had a 'fixer,' someone who swept in and took care of … well, any problem that needed to go away. It was plausible, and in certain elite circles, it was the way things had always been done.

As I allowed the notion to marinate in my mind, I decided to pay another visit to Alexander tomorrow. Tonight, I wanted nothing more than to snuggle up with Luka and relax. The thought of it brought a smile to my face, as did the thought of Giovanni returning home tomorrow.

I unlocked the car door and opened it, tossing my handbag onto the passenger seat. I was about to step inside when I felt something on the back of my neck.

Someone's breath—hot and steamy—and I knew I wasn't alone.

I'd been so caught up in my murder theories, I hadn't paid enough attention to my surroundings, a big, big mistake on my part.

As I lunged for the gun inside my handbag, I felt a sharp pain on the side of my head, strong and numbing. Blood, wet and sticky, trickled down the side of my cheek, and I jerked back, preparing to headbutt my attacker. No sooner had I done it, my head began spinning, and then, everything went black.

CHAPTER 29

"I tell you what—this is the exact reason I have never been able to accept Georgiana's line of work. Just look at what happened tonight, would you? She could have been killed, for heaven's sake, and for what? It doesn't make much sense to solve a person's murder if you get yourself murdered in the process. As soon as Georgiana wakes up, I'll tell her as much. It's time she stopped this nonsense."

My eyes flashed open, coming to rest on the woman who'd been airing her unsolicited opinions—my mother. She was standing with her back to me, hands on her hips. In front of her was Giovanni, who looked like he was at a loss for words, which, for him, was uncommon.

He didn't seem to know what to say. Or maybe he did, and he'd decided it was better to keep quiet, give her time to calm down.

Either way, my head was throbbing, and I was in no mood to deal with her theatrics.

"Mom," I said. "Let's not talk about this right now, okay?"

My mother whipped around, shuffling my way, then collapsing over my body, throwing her arms around me.

"Oh, my dear, you gave us such a scare," she said.

"Everything's going to be all right. I'm fine."

I told myself I was fine, at least.

I attempted to smile at Giovanni, but given the numbing sensation I was feeling on the right side of my face, I imagined the expression I made was more clownlike than cheery.

"I thought you weren't supposed to be back in Cambria until tomorrow," I said.

"It is tomorrow, *cara mia*. The moment I received word about what happened to you last night, I flew straight home."

What did he mean, it was tomorrow?

It seemed like hours had gone by, not a whole day.

I turned toward the window and noticed the sunlight's attempt to dance its way through the cracks and crevices of the shuttered window blinds.

Given what I was wearing and the sterileness of the room, I was in the hospital, though I had no recollection of how I came to be there.

"How long have I been out," I asked, "or asleep … or whatever?"

"You had minor surgery," my mother said. "On your head."

"I did?"

"You sure did, and then one of the nurses gave you something for the pain, and something else to help you sleep, and you've been out ever since. No doubt you needed the rest. Maybe it will help you get your head on straight and rethink your career choice."

"Mom … not now, okay?"

"If not now, when? I'm just saying what everyone else is thinking."

"Everyone else … like who?"

"Now, let's see … in the waiting room is your stepfather, of course, your Aunt Laura, your sister, and Foley and Whitlock."

She tapped a foot to the floor. "Who am I missing? Ahh, yes. Simone and Hunter are there too."

"It's just a little bump on the head," I said. "I don't know what everyone is getting so worked up about."

My mother huffed an irritated sigh, looked at me, and said, "A little bump on the head? I should think not. Here, sit up if you can. I want to show you something."

I propped myself up a bit more, which didn't make much difference, watching as my mother fiddled inside her purse. A moment later she pulled out a compact mirror, opened it, and turned it in my direction. At the same time, Giovanni reached out as if trying to intercept the mirror before I had the chance to see my reflection, but she was determined—and, therefore, a lot faster.

As my reflection came into view, I leaned closer to the mirror, assessing the damage, and there was plenty of it. The side of my head where I'd been struck had been shaved, and a five-inch gash remained. It had been stitched up, making it look even worse.

"Does that look like a little bump on the head to you?" my mother asked.

"I ... I don't know what to say. I remember being attacked, but I had no idea I was hurt this bad."

Giovanni stepped in front of my mother. "You can put the mirror away now, Darlene. I believe Georgiana's seen enough."

"I ... well, I just wanted to make sure she understands the extent of her injuries."

She snapped the compact closed, slipping it back inside her purse, looking sheepish. Her cheeks were flushed, tinged with red, no doubt in reaction to Giovanni's tone. While he'd always respected her, his respect was secondary to his protectiveness of me. His tone had conveyed a clear message—she'd pushed me enough for today.

He faced me, entwining his hand with mine. "Do you remember what happened last night?"

It was fuzzy, at best.

"I remember locking the office door and walking to my car," I said. "I'm almost always aware of what's going on around me, but last night, I was in my head, instead of focusing on my surroundings like I should have been."

"It's all right."

"No, it isn't. I put myself in this situation by taking this case. I'm supposed to be ready for it, ready for anything, and I wasn't."

He winked and said, "A fall into a pit, a gain in your wit."

"Chinese proverb?"

He nodded. "We learn from our mistakes—not that I'm saying you made one."

"You're right. I didn't make one. I made several."

A woman ambled into the room, humming as she carried a tray of food. My mother held out her hands, intercepting the tray before it reached me.

"Just stopping by to bring Miss Georgiana some lunch," the woman said.

My mother took one look at the tray's contents and scowled. "Ehh, thank you."

The woman nodded and left the room, at which time my mother tossed the entire tray of food into the trash. Before I could get a word out, she grabbed an insulated bag off a coat rack and unzipped it, pulling out an egg-based Buddha bowl. I had to admit, it looked delicious.

"Your Aunt Laura made this for you this morning. Still warm too."

She handed it to me along with some silverware, a napkin, and an orange-flavored drink with electrolytes. I accepted the offerings, setting the items to the side until I finished the conversation.

"As I was saying before, when I got to my car, I tossed my handbag onto the passenger seat. I was just about to get in when I felt someone's breath on the back of my neck."

"Did you get a look at your attacker, by chance?" Giovanni asked.

"I didn't, and because my gun was in my handbag, I had to think fast."

"What did you do?"

"I headbutted my attacker, slammed the back of my head onto him as hard as I could. That's the last thing I remember."

"You said your handbag was on the passenger seat?" Giovanni asked.

"Yeah, why?"

"When Foley and Whitlock searched your car, they didn't find a handbag."

The thought of my bag being stolen infuriated me.

First, I hadn't had the chance to go over the file Barbara gave me. Now, the file was gone, along with what could be valuable clues relating to Noelle's murder.

Second, the stolen handbag was a vintage Chanel tote, one that had belonged to my grandmother.

"Do you know why anyone would take your handbag?" Giovanni asked.

I made one more attempt at sitting higher up in the bed, and I was a lot more successful the second time around. "I do. I had two important file folders inside the bag. One contained everything I'd gathered about the case so far—all my notes. I was planning to go over the case file last night to see if there were any clues I may have overlooked."

"And the second?"

"Noelle hired a private investigator to find one of the women who'd visited the women's center and then disappeared. The investigator she hired couldn't find her, but he still put together a file on his investigation. That was in my bag too."

"What's this about a woman?"

I turned, noticing Foley had entered the room.

"I went to the women's center today … I mean, yesterday, and

I spoke to Barbara. She's worked as the manager of the center ever since it opened. Barbara told me about a woman named Dawn who arrived at the center in bad shape."

"How bad of shape are we talking?"

"She'd been severely beaten. They were trying to get her to talk, to tell them what happened. I think the pressure of admitting what happened and who hurt her was too much, and she fled the center. No one has seen her since. Noelle was worried about Dawn, so she hired a private investigator to find her."

"Why would Noelle get involved to such a degree?" Foley asked. "From what we've been told, it wasn't like her to do that—for her own security."

"I believe there's a connection between Dawn and the reason Noelle was murdered. What's more, Noelle told Zoey she recognized Dawn. She'd seen her before at the tennis club *before* she was assaulted."

"Did Zoey say anything else?"

"There was an argument in the club parking lot between Dawn and someone else, but we don't know who Dawn was arguing with, or why."

Foley ran a hand across his bald head, his expression one of shock and amazement. "Well, Georgiana, I think you've made the biggest breakthrough in the case so far."

"I do too. I just wish I had that file."

"Yeah, there's a good chance it was taken for a reason."

"If my attacker thinks taking it will change anything, he's mistaken. I know the name of the private investigator she hired. As soon as I get out of here, I'm going to go see him."

"Do you think you were attacked because of the file Barbara gave you?"

"I think it's a combination of things. Someone is trying to send me a warning. And they either wanted to get their hands on the file in the process, or they were trying to find out how much I know. Ask me, they're scared, which tells me, we're getting close to nailing this guy."

Foley leaned against the wall. "You were hit by a blunt object of some kind. If you blacked out, your attacker could have finished the job. Wonder why he didn't?"

My mother raised a finger. "Haven't you spoken to Simone yet?"

"No, she was on the phone when I got here," Foley said. "Why?"

"Simone left her phone in the kitchen at the office last night, and she went back to get it. When she turned into the parking lot, she saw someone in a hoodie standing next to Georgiana's car. He looked toward her, and then he took off. When she pulled up next to the car, she saw Georgiana. By then, the guy was long gone."

"I hurt him when I slammed into him," I said. "I know because he groaned. I'm not sure how much of an impact I made, though."

"Did you get any indication as to his size?" Foley asked.

"He seemed taller than me. When I rammed into him with my head, it felt like I'd hit his chest, and I was in two-inch heels, so that would make him at least six feet tall, I'd say."

"Good to know."

"As soon as I'm given the green light to get out of here, I plan to speak to every person who has ties to the tennis club, try to dig up possible motives for Noelle's murder."

Wagging a finger in the air, my mother shook her head. "Oh, no you're not! No, siree! You need rest and lots of it. It's time you left the policing to Foley and Whitlock. Let them catch this guy."

Not wanting to incite an argument while Giovanni and Foley were in the room, I said nothing, my inner dialogue telling me what I couldn't tell her—Noelle's killer may have slowed me down, but he hadn't stopped me.

The next time he came for me, I'd be ready.

CHAPTER 30

The next morning, Giovanni entered our house looking chuffed, sporting a big, wide smile on his face. He'd come bearing gifts, which I was happy to accept. In one hand, he held a drink tray with a couple of lattes. In the other was a department store bag.

"What do you have there?" I asked.

He set everything down on the counter, pulled one of the lattes out of its cardboard drink holder, and handed it to me. "First, let's get some caffeine into you."

"Good idea."

Over the next few minutes, we chitchatted, and my eyes couldn't help but wander to the bag on the counter, contemplating what might be inside.

When my patience was all but spent, an entire minute later, I pointed at the bag. "So … what's in there?"

He laughed, making a cute quip about how childlike I was when it came to presents. He grabbed the bag and handed it to me.

"You are beautiful to me inside and out," he said. "They could have shaved your entire head, and it wouldn't make a difference. You'd still be the most stunning woman I've ever seen."

"I ... thank you. I'll admit I've been avoiding looking in the mirror. How am I supposed to meet with people and expect them to focus on me instead of the huge gash on my head?"

He gestured at the bag. "This might help."

Curious, I pulled the bag to me and reached inside, pulling out an adorable light-pink wig. It was shaped in a bob style—the most perfect, thoughtful gift he could have given me right now.

"Do you like it?" he asked.

"I *love* it," I said.

"Given how much effort you put into your wardrobe, I knew you'd want to step out of the house in style."

"Does this mean you're on board with me stepping out? After what my mother said, I've been wondering if the rest of you think I should be sitting this one out too."

"I don't believe anyone else has given it a moment's thought. Your mother said what she did out of fear. I imagine what happened to you scared her. It may have even triggered her, thinking about your father, and the fact he was murdered doing the same line of work that you do."

It was something I should have realized before and hadn't. Now, I understood the words she'd said to me a lot more than I had in the hospital room. I needed to be more sympathetic, think about it from her perspective.

"You're right," I said. "I should have considered where she was coming from, and while I want to put her at ease, being a private investigator is fulfilling to me. And yeah, maybe I'm a little banged up from the attack, but I'm invested in this case. I'm not about to leave it to Whitlock and Foley to find Noelle's killer."

Giovanni offered me a nod, saying, "I don't believe you'd ever sit on the sidelines unless you had no other choice. Still, I'm concerned for your safety on this one. Speaking of which, I have a proposition."

"I'm listening."

"I'd like to accompany you on your interviews. And before

you say anything, I know you can take care of yourself. I'm offering added support. It will give me great peace of mind."

It would give my mother peace of mind as well.

"I don't want you to worry," I said. "I don't want my mother to worry, either. But this job, being a private investigator, it's a part of who I am, a part of the air I breathe. I wouldn't be me without it."

"Deep down, your mother knows you'll never abandon your passion, and while we're on the topic, I would never ask it of you."

"I know you wouldn't."

What he was asking was fair, and as I gave it some thought, I tried to consider how I'd feel if the roles were reversed. Giovanni was the toughest, most formidable man I'd ever known, but part of me was still nervous when he flew home for his family meetings. Sure, nowadays the families were at peace, for the most part, but I was smart enough to know that sometimes peace didn't always last.

"Tagging along with me might not be as interesting as you think," I said. "But if it's what you want, I'm fine with it."

"It is what I want, and don't sell yourself short. There's never been a dull moment between us since the day we met."

"Speaking of the day we met, once this case is finished, I'm not taking on another murder investigation until after we're married. I want to focus on us and our wedding."

His smile told me he was pleased with my decision.

It was the right one.

But before my focus could shift to happier days ahead, I had a murder to solve.

CHAPTER 31

I was sitting in Alexander Beaumont's study with Giovanni, waiting for Alexander to finish the call he'd just taken behind closed doors in his office. A few minutes passed and then he joined us, his eyes laser-focused on my wig.

"New hairstyle, I see," he said.

"I needed a change," I said.

"Can't say I've known many women to don such a color, but you, my dear, you pull it off well."

"Thank you."

Compliment aside, he shifted his attention to Giovanni. "You have a familiar look about you. Have we met somewhere before?"

"I don't believe so."

"What's your name, if you don't mind me asking?"

"Giovanni Luciana."

Alexander ran a hand along his jawline, repeating the surname under his breath. *"Luciana* … might be a longshot, but you wouldn't happen to be related to Matteo Luciana, would you? He's of the New York Luciana family, lives on the family estate, if I'm not mistaken."

"Matteo is my uncle."

"Ahh, yes. You look a lot like him."

"How is it the two of you are acquainted?"

"I own several homes, one in the heart of New York City. I spend the fall season there. When I'm visiting, I participate in a weekly poker game with some buddies of mine. Your uncle has attended a few times. Nice fellow."

"Small world we live in," I said.

"Small indeed, Miss Germaine." He flicked a finger left to right. "So … how do the two of you know each other?"

"Giovanni is my fiancé," I said.

"Ahh, and does he accompany you during your investigations often?"

"Sometimes."

I leaned back and looked Alexander in the eye. If he had anything to do with my assault, nothing in his placid demeanor indicated as much. Then again, he struck me as a man who had plenty to hide and was good at hiding it when it suited him.

As I thought about the best way to catch him off guard, an idea came to mind. I grabbed my wig, yanking it off my head, a gesture that came as a surprise to both men. It was just the reaction I wanted.

Alexander slapped a hand to his lips. "The new hair, I understand now. What happened to you?"

"Someone assaulted me as I was leaving my workplace."

He glanced at Giovanni, offering a slight nod, suggesting he had a better understanding of why I wasn't alone today.

"The man who attacked you, did you get a good look at him, at least?" Alexander asked.

"I never said a *man* attacked me."

"I … I, well, I just assumed. Are you all right?"

"A little banged up, but I'm fine."

"Any reason why someone would do such a thing? I mean, if I had to guess, I'd say it must have something to do with your murder investigation. Are you getting any closer to solving it?"

"I am, and I'm positive the incident is related. My handbag was stolen in the process, along with a couple of important files."

"'And did these files contain sensitive information relevant to your case?"

I nodded. "Are you aware of the Ophelia Albrecht Center? It's a women's center founded by Dominic and Noelle."

"I was not made aware of its founders until after her death. There was an article about the center in the paper. I knew of the center, of course. I just wasn't aware of Noelle's association with it. I've heard great things about the place. It's made a big difference in many women's lives over the years."

"In the weeks before Noelle died, a woman named Dawn Salisbury came to the center seeking help. Does her name sound familiar to you?"

He shook his head. "Any reason why it should?"

"When Dawn arrived at the center, she had been badly beaten. Noelle was able to talk Dawn into getting her injuries looked at by a doctor. Not long after, she fled the center."

Alexander narrowed his eyes, looking at me like he was trying to determine my angle, the reason I was relaying Dawn's story, and what it had to do with him.

"I feel for any woman in such a position, but tell me, Miss Germaine, why share what happened to this woman with me?"

He was about to see the correlation.

"I believe Dawn fled the women's center because Noelle recognized her or vice versa," I said. "Noelle remembered seeing Dawn before, arguing with someone in the parking lot of the tennis club."

"Strange coincidence. Do you know with whom she was arguing?"

"Not yet, but I intend to find out. I plan to stop at the club today, talk to a few people, and see if they have any security cameras. If there's footage of the argument, I need to see it."

"I suppose whether or not there's footage depends on when the argument took place."

I crossed my arms, confused by his comment. "Why does that matter?"

"There might not be any footage."

"Why not?"

"A couple of months ago, we had a company meeting with the club's investors. The focus of the meeting was on cutting costs. The club is profitable, but profits can always be better. We discussed the ridiculous amount of money we've been paying each month to our security service. We've never had a single break-in or theft … well, aside from Owen's misconduct."

"Are you saying you canceled the security service?"

"We did. In saying that, we're aware it's good measure to have some form of security. But given how much more convenient technology has become, we figured why use an expensive service when we could install and monitor security cameras ourselves, right from our phones."

"You still have security cameras then, right?"

He nodded. "We have them. The reason they won't be of any use to you is because we installed them in front of the main entrance of the club. Monitoring the parking lot is of no concern to us."

It wasn't what I wanted to hear, and the timing seemed convenient.

Perhaps a little *too* convenient.

"I suppose I'll need to figure out who was arguing with Dawn some other way," I said.

"You must have someone in mind. Otherwise, why would you have told me the story at all?"

He didn't miss a beat, always assessing my motives.

It bugged me.

At the same time, I found his attention to every detail of our conversation impressive. I was certain he knew who I suspected

had been arguing with Dawn, even if I didn't know the
reason why.

"Given your nephew's misbehavior, it's easy for me to suspect
he could have been the person talking to Dawn that day," I said.

Alexander offered a slight shrug, pausing, and then saying,
"Theft and abuse are two entirely different things, are they not? If
you're right, and I don't believe you are, I wouldn't know
anything about it."

For a moment, I looked at him, and he looked at me, neither
of us speaking. I'd paid close attention to his demeanor when I
voiced my opinion about Owen. He showed indifference,
nothing more.

Maybe he'd had a lot of practice when it came to accusations
pointed at himself and members of his family, whether true
or not.

"If I may," he said, "we can agree on one thing—my nephew
has grossly mismanaged money coming into the club. It's
important to note that he's been dealt with and will be working
at the club no longer. I can assure you, as long as I draw breath,
he will never again work in a position that involves our family's
money in any way. As to your feelings on Owen speaking to the
woman in question, even if it was him, he's no abuser of
women."

Prior to what he'd learned about Owen in the last week, he
may have said the same thing about his thievery.

It was possible he didn't know his nephew as well as he
thought he did.

Or he did know him well, and he was lying to me.

"Dawn hasn't been seen since she left the women's center," I
said. "Noelle hired a private investigator to find her, which was
an uncharacteristic thing for her to do. It makes me wonder *why*
she did it."

"I'm guessing the investigation into Dawn's whereabouts was
not a success or you would have more answers than questions.

Pity Noelle didn't hire you. I've no doubt your search for the missing woman would have been far more successful."

"You're right. The investigator never found her. I was given a copy of the file he turned over to Noelle with his findings, or lack thereof."

"A file that was stolen, correct?"

I nodded.

"Were you able to look through it beforehand?" he asked.

First, he'd questioned me about whether I'd gotten a good look at my attacker. Now, he was asking if I'd seen the file.

Suspicious.

"I'll find Dawn, with or without the file," I said.

"I have no doubt." He reached for the teapot next to him, pouring himself a cup. He took a sip, frowning as he muttered something about the tea going cold.

"You know from our last visit that I'm a frank man," Alexander said. "I'll admit, as much as I enjoy our visits, my patience is running thin. If there's a point to all of this, beyond what you've already said, you best get on with it."

"All right, I will. I believe there's a connection between Noelle's death and Dawn's disappearance, as I'm sure by now you've realized. The way I see it, the person who assaulted Dawn was someone Noelle knew, and the tennis club seems to be at the center of it all."

"You may be right. Time will tell."

"Here's how I see the chain of events. Noelle saw Dawn arguing with someone from the club. At some point after that, Dawn was assaulted. Noelle assumed she knew who did it. She confronted the person, possibly even making a threat to share what she knew, and she was murdered for it."

"All good theories, until they're proven."

"I plan to speak with Owen."

"Owen is unreachable at present."

Even more suspicious.

"I don't understand," I said.

"Upon visiting him at his home, or I should say, entering his home without his knowledge, I discovered an assortment of drugs. It explains his actions, his need to steal from the club. He was confronted and given an ultimatum—enter drug rehab or be cut from my will."

"I'm guessing the rehab facility does not allow visitors, which is why he's unable to speak with me, right?"

"You are correct. He isn't supposed to have any contact with anyone outside of the facility. I have some pull, however, and if you permit me, I will speak to him about our conversation today … *only* if he's of the right mind to receive it."

I appreciated his offer, and given I had no choice, I took him up on it.

I left with one question: was Alexander sincere in his offer to help me, or was he trying to keep Owen from me while he cleaned up his mess?

CHAPTER 32

Austin Cole had his boots kicked up over the top of his desk when Giovanni and I entered his office. He glanced our way, tipping his cowboy hat as he came to a sitting position and said, "Hello there, what can I do for you?"

We took a seat, and I got right to the point.

"I understand you were hired by Noelle Winters to find Dawn Salisbury," I said.

"You heard right, though finding the girl wasn't much of a success. Why do you ask?"

"I was hired by one of Noelle's friends to investigate her murder."

He raised a brow. "You're Georgiana Germaine, aren't ya?"

"I am."

"Nice to meet you in person. I've heard a lot about your detective agency, which is takin' a bit of my business, I might add."

Perhaps if he was more successful locating the people he was hired to find, his business wouldn't be lacking, though I didn't say as much.

He turned toward Giovanni. "And you … do you work for Miss Germaine?"

Giovanni grinned. "In a way."

"Well, what can I do for ya? Guessin' you're not here to hire me."

He slapped a hand to his knee and laughed.

"I believe there's a connection between Dawn and the reason Noelle's murder," I said.

"How so?"

"For starters, I was given a copy of your case file. Within hours of receiving the file, it was stolen from me."

"Don't know why it would be. Nothin' in the file was incriminating."

"Are you sure about that?"

"As sure as I can be."

"I'd like to know about your interactions with Noelle and how she came to hire you."

"Oh, the hiring part's easy. I took tennis lessons from her."

"*You* took tennis lessons?"

"I take it you don't think I look the part."

"I apologize. I didn't mean to be rude."

He swished a hand through the air. "Truth is, I never thought I'd swing a racket in my life."

"So, why did you?"

"To impress my girl. She plays, and I thought if I learned the basics, I could surprise her on her birthday."

"What a sweet thing to do. Was she surprised?"

Austin sighed, scratching a finger behind his ear. "We … ahh, broke up. Well, that is to say, we're takin' some time apart. I messed things up, but I'm tryin' awful hard to get her back."

Several moments of awkward silence later, I said, "What did Noelle say to you when she hired you?"

"She asked me for my discretion, said somethin' about how

her family wouldn't approve of what she was doin' if they found out."

"What were her reasons for hiring you?"

"She was worried about Dawn, said she was being abused, and she thought she knew who was abusing her, but she wanted to be sure."

"Did she give you a name?"

"No, ma'am."

"Did she say how she knew who was abusing her?"

"She witnessed an altercation between Dawn and the suspected abuser."

"Yeah, in the parking lot at the tennis club."

His eyes widened. "That so? She didn't tell me it happened at the club."

I wondered why she'd left that part out.

"If she wanted you to find Dawn, why not give you all the information she could, starting with whom she suspected of abuse?" I asked.

"My opinion? She didn't want to name anyone until she was able to prove it one way another. When she came to my office, she was worried, real worried. I'm guessin' she thought once I found Dawn, she'd have the answers she was hoping to find."

"Speaking of Dawn, what can you tell me about your investigation?"

"Not much, I'm afraid. When I went to her house, the door was unlocked, so I did what any investigator in my position would do—I went inside. The place was a mess, and it looked like she'd just stepped out for a moment, like she would be back any time. Found clothes in all the drawers, suitcases in the closet, and her car was there too."

"When you searched the house, did you find any clues as to her whereabouts?"

"Nothing solid, no."

I failed to believe he did an entire search of her place and left without a single, solitary lead.

"How long have you had your detective agency?" I asked.

"I see where you're goin' with your question. And yeah, I'll admit it, I have a lot to learn. Noelle was my third client, but the first who'd asked me to find a missing person. My other two cases were easy. Just had to follow the spouses of my clients, take pictures, and report back."

"I see."

"I did my best to find Dawn."

When it came to doing one's best, we had differing opinions. If it had been me, I wouldn't have stopped looking until she was found.

Realizing I wasn't getting anywhere with our conversation, I stood, thanking him for taking the time to speak to me.

As Giovanni and I walked to the door, Austin shouted out, "You know the worst part of Dawn's case?"

I turned. "What's that?"

"It's bad enough for a man to lay a hand on a woman, but what kind of man beats a woman when she's pregnant?"

CHAPTER 33

What kind of man beats a woman when she's pregnant ...

I'd never fully understood why Noelle hired a private investigator to find Dawn or why her situation was different than the other women who came to the women's center, until now. Sure, I'd started connecting the dots between Dawn, Noelle, and the tennis club ... but learning Dawn was pregnant?

It changed everything.

Before I left Austin's office, I asked him how he knew about Dawn's baby. When Noelle took Dawn to be looked over by a doctor, Dawn asked Noelle to sit in the waiting room while she met with him. And for good reason. The doctor ran a few tests, and upon discovering the pregnancy, he asked Dawn if she knew she was with child. She did, and she admitted she'd only agreed to go to the hospital to make sure the baby was all right.

At first, Noelle knew nothing about Dawn's pregnancy. But once the doctor learned Dawn had left the women's center and was missing, his conscience got the better of him, and he couldn't keep quiet. He shared news of the pregnancy with Noelle, hoping she would do what she could to find Dawn.

That's when she hired a private investigator.

As I thought about Dawn and what the odds were she was still alive, Giovanni pulled to a stop in front of her apartment.

Turning toward him, I said, "I'm not sure what to expect. The apartment could be rented to someone else by now."

He nodded. "Let's find out."

We exited the car, and as we approached the front door, I noticed a woman eyeing me from the next building over, the look on her face one of skepticism. We made eye contact. She was around my age I guessed and on the shorter side with curly, red hair and matching eyeglasses.

Wagging a finger at us, she speedwalked our way, her bright, flowy, multicolored dress swishing from side to side as she shouted, "You two. Stop right there!"

We did as instructed and waited for her to catch up to us.

When she got to the door, she said, "This is a private residential community," she said. "I'll not have you or anyone else nosing around. And just so we're clear, I want no part of your news article or podcast or whatever you people are here for, either."

"We're not reporters, and we're not with the paper or a radio show," I said.

"Well then, who are ya? And what's your business here?"

I made the introductions, explaining who we were and why we were there, adding, "We weren't even sure coming here was a good idea. Dawn's been missing for several weeks now, long enough that I expect her place might be rented to someone else."

"Dawn's paid through the end of the month. As far as I'm concerned, the unit is still hers until I have no choice but to rent it to someone else."

"I take it you're the apartment manager?"

"And her friend, I'd like to think, which is why I'm so protective about people coming around, poking in business that isn't theirs."

"All we're trying to do is find her."

She studied me like she was trying to decide whether to

believe me or not. "You aren't the first ones to claim you care about Dawn's whereabouts. Betting you won't be the last either."

Giovanni smiled at the woman. "We've just introduced ourselves, but you haven't done the same. Miss …?"

"Ramona Olson."

"Ramona, what a lovely name."

She moved a hand to her hip, brow furrowed. "Well … you're a charming one, aren't ya? Let me tell you a little something about me. I know all about men like you, men who'll say anything to get what they want. Let's get one thing straight—

I'm not the gullible type."

Giovanni tipped his head back and laughed, and I couldn't help but do the same.

"Why are you laughing?" Ramona asked. "What's so funny?"

"You're one feisty woman, Ramona," I said. "I can relate."

She elbowed me in the side. "Us broads have to be if we wanna make it in this world."

"I agree."

"Now that the pleasantries are out of the way, what is it you want?"

Straight to the point.

I liked it.

"I was hoping we could take a quick peek inside Dawn's apartment," I said. "I'm looking for any clues to assist me in locating her."

"You ever consider she up and left because she wanted to leave this place, start over, and the like? What makes you think she wants to be found?"

"If she's alive, there's a good chance she's on the run, that she left because she didn't think she had any other choice."

"Now just hold on a minute. Why'd you say what you just did … *if* she's alive? Why wouldn't she be?"

I put the comment to the side for now, changing subjects.

"You said the two of you are friends," I said. "What do you know about the man she was dating?"

"What man? There's no man. None I've ever seen around here, anyway." There was a long pause, and then, "Except …"

She tapped a finger to her lips.

"Except what?" I asked.

"A few times, right before she took off, Dawn didn't come home after work. I know because the lights in her place didn't come on. I'm up at the crack of dawn, making the most of my day from the start, and a few times I noticed she got home at six, seven in the morning. She'd go into her apartment, change into her work clothes, and leave about an hour later. Always wondered where she'd been all night."

"You didn't ask her?"

"Didn't want to seem nosy."

She may not have wanted to *seem* nosy, but it was obvious she kept tabs on her neighbors—or Dawn, at least.

"When's the last time you saw or talked to Dawn?" I asked.

"Let's see now … would have been about a week before Noelle Winters reported her missing. She stopped by here, looking for Dawn … you know, before she was murdered."

"What did the two of you talk about?"

"She asked if I'd seen Dawn, or if I knew where she was, and I told her I did not. She seemed real worried, kept saying Dawn was missing, and she needed to find her. Then she left."

As much as I liked where the conversation was going, I needed to get inside Dawn's apartment, and I hoped Ramona had warmed up to the idea.

"Would it be possible to have a look inside Dawn's apartment?" I asked.

"Even if I wanted to let ya'll in, I can't. Privacy and all. Wouldn't be right, and besides, I should be getting back to the office."

Before I had a chance to reply, she'd turned, offering us a slight wave as she trotted off.

If I wanted to get inside Dawn's place, I had to think fast.

"Hey, Ramona, I need to tell you something, but it needs to stay between us," I said.

Knowing how attentive she was to Dawn's goings-on, and I bet every resident who lived in the community—I was sure she'd jump at the chance to hear a bit of juicy gossip.

And I was right.

She marched back our way, saying, "Oh, I'm good at keeping secrets. I know so many things about the people who live here."

I had no doubt.

"Before I say anything more, I'd like for us to make a deal," I said.

"What kind of deal?"

"If I tell you why I believe Dawn is missing and why she's in danger, will you give me fifteen minutes inside her apartment? No one has to know you let me in. It will stay between us. You have my word."

She tapped a shoe to the pavement, mulling over my offer. "Your word means nothing. I don't even know ya. On a scale of one to ten, just how juicy are we talking?"

I shot her a wink. "Ten juicy."

"If it's a ten, you get ten minutes inside her place, and I'll be coming with you, to supervise, make sure everything's above board." Thumbing at Giovanni, she said, "Just you, though. Not him."

"You have yourself a deal."

Ramona glanced around, making sure we were alone, and then she leaned in close. "Go on, then … this better be good."

"Right before Dawn disappeared, she checked into the women's center that Noelle Winters founded. She'd been badly beaten. Noelle convinced her to see a doctor. Not long after, Dawn left the center, and she hasn't been seen since."

Shaking her head, Ramona said, "Why didn't you tell me this in the first place?"

"Oh, I'm not finished. You wanted a ten juicy, and here it is … during the doctor's assessment, he discovered something about Dawn."

"Something like …?"

"Dawn is pregnant."

CHAPTER 34

Dawn's apartment was in disarray when we entered, and not in a ransacked kind of way. It was clear Dawn was a messy person. There were fast-food wrappers on the sofa, empty soda cans on the coffee table, which had a broken leg that had been duct-taped to keep it in place. The apartment didn't appear to have been dusted or vacuumed in ages. Given its messy state, I was shocked as I entered the kitchen. It was pristine.

Turning toward Ramona, I said, "I don't get it. How could her entire place be a cluttered mess and the kitchen be tidy? It's like two different types of people live here."

Ramona offered me a sheepish grin. "Oh, well, you see … I did a look-see through the kitchen window after Dawn had been gone for a week. There were a bunch of dishes piled up in the sink. None of them had been rinsed off, and food was stuck to them. Food that was … well, starting to have bacterial growth, if you know what I mean. I was sure the place stunk to high heaven, and given the residents on the first floor all use the same hallway, I started to worry they'd notice."

"Did you clean Dawn's kitchen?"

"Between us, I sure did."

She pointed to a note beneath a dog magnet on the refrigerator door.

It read:

Hello, Dawn,

I was doing a routine inspection and noticed your dishes needed to be done. I hope you don't mind, but as you have been away for some time now, I thought it best to wash them for you. We wouldn't want the other residents to complain now, would we?

Your friend,

Ramona Olson

Apartment Manager, but you know that already

P.S. Stop by the office for a chat any time.

As much as Ramona labeled herself as one of Dawn's friends, I was of the notion that Ramona *wished* to be Dawn's friend, but in all likelihood, she wasn't even an acquaintance. I felt for her. She struck me as the type of woman who was often misunderstood—much because of her strong, quirky personality.

For the next several minutes I searched through kitchen drawers and cabinets, moved things around, looking for clues, finding none. In the bedroom, I found Dawn's suitcases, just like Austin had, but upon closer inspection of her open dresser drawers, they were sparse, like things were missing. Perhaps Dawn had returned home for a short time, loading several things into a duffel bag before she took off.

Ramona entered the room. "What do you think? Anything?"

I pointed at the top drawer. "There are only a few pairs of

panties in this drawer, and a few bras in the next. Women never own just a few pairs of panties. It doesn't make sense."

"I'll be right back." Ramona marched down the hall, returning a minute later. "Washer and dryer are empty, and I don't see a laundry basket full of clothes anywhere around here."

"It's possible Dawn packed a few things before she took off."

"I take self-defense classes two nights a week. If she was here during that time, she could have come and gone without me seeing her."

"Are there any security cameras in the community?"

Ramona laughed. "Security cameras? I can't even get them to spring for a vending machine, which the guy who owns this place would make money on, I might add."

I spent the next several minutes looking around the rest of Dawn's room. In one of the drawers, I found a notebook with the word POETRY on the front. I flipped through its pages, noting several handwritten poems, my eyes wide as they came to rest on the title of the last poem in the book. It was titled: "Winter Is Like a Trickster, Full of Lies."

A chill ran up my spine, as I realized the title of the poem was the exact words Noelle had spoken to me in my dream. Aside from the title, the poem hadn't been written yet. Even so, it told me one thing—I was in the exact place I needed to be.

I entered the bathroom and looked around.

"Hey, Ramona, did Dawn wear a lot of makeup?"

"More than most women I know. Why?"

"There's not much of it in these drawers."

"How odd."

Odd, indeed.

In the wastebasket, I noticed a crumpled-up napkin with writing on it. I leaned over, fishing it out. The napkin appeared to have gotten wet at some point, blurring part of what had been written. All I could make out was 5 Salt.

I grabbed my phone and made a call.

"How's it going?" Hunter asked when she answered.

"It's going," I said. "I need a favor."

"Name it."

"I'm in Dawn's apartment, and I found a napkin in the trash that's been written on, but part of the word is blurred out. I'm thinking it might be an address. I can make out 5 Salt, but that's it. Will you search for any addresses around here that have the word *salt* in them, and then take those addresses and cross-reference them with everyone we've spoken to during this case?"

"I'll get on it right now."

I thanked her and ended the call.

"I believe I'm done here, Ramona," I said. "Thank you. I know you agreed to ten minutes, but you've allowed me to look around a lot longer."

She gave me a wide smile and said, "Aww, it's nothing. What are rules for if ya can't bend them once in a while, right?"

"Right."

"Now that you told me the scoop, I have to say, I'm worried. If there's anything else I can do, anything at all, you just buzz on over here."

As we stepped outside, I said, "Is there anything else you can tell me about Dawn before I go? Anything to help me understand her better?"

"Sure."

For the next several minutes, I listened as Ramona went over Dawn's daily routine in excruciating detail, including how she dressed, what days she worked, what days she had off, the type of food she liked to eat, among other things. As she wrapped up, I received a text message from Hunter, and with it, a shock to my system.

"Is everything okay?" Ramona asked.

"No, I don't think so. But never mind that for now. What did you just say?"

"I asked you if everything was okay."

"Before that."

"Oh, I said sorry for assuming you were a reporter like the last guy who was here, trying to get into Dawn's apartment. Thought he could get into the place by offering me a piece of Bubble Magic. Who likes that old stuff nowadays?"

CHAPTER 35

Heidi Fletcher had large, doe eyes, a petite frame, and a sweet smile when she met me at the door.

"You're Clark's wife, aren't you?" I asked.

"Yes, I am. How do you know Clark?"

"He and I have spoken a few times over the past week. I'm investigating the murder of Noelle Winters."

"Oh, right. He told me about you."

"Is he here right now, by chance? I stopped by Royal Palms, and they told me he had the afternoon off."

"He's at a doctor's appointment."

"Nothing serious, I hope."

"Oh, no. Just a routine physical."

"I was wondering, can we talk?"

"I … I guess so."

"Give me just one minute, okay? I just need to run back to my car for a second."

She nodded. "Sure, I'll leave the door open. We can talk in the living room. It's straight down the hall."

I turned, walking back to the car, where Giovanni was waiting.

"What have you found out?" he asked.

"Nothing yet. She's agreed to let me come in and talk to her, and I think I'd get a lot further if I did it alone."

"Where's Clark?"

"She said he's at a doctor's appointment."

"Do you believe her?"

"I don't know."

He tapped a thumb to the steering wheel. "Keep your phone in hand, and if you suspect things are about to go sideways, text me. I'll be right there."

I nodded and headed inside, stepping into the living room where Heidi was moving a half-knitted blanket off the couch, giving us both a place to sit down.

Her cheery disposition had changed.

Now she looked nervous, her expression laced with concern and worry.

I took a seat, wasting no time in getting to the point of my visit.

"I've been investigating Noelle's murder for several days now, and I believe I know who murdered her and why," I said.

She bit her lip. "Why are you telling me this?"

"I believe Clark murdered Noelle."

"I can't believe … I don't … I don't understand. Noelle and Clark were friends. How could you say such a thing?"

"Has Clark always been faithful to you?"

"Our marriage has had its ups and downs. He loves me, and I love him."

It was a polite way of admitting he hadn't always been faithful.

"Infidelity isn't love," I said.

"Every relationship dynamic is different. What does my husband's fidelity have to do with your accusation?"

She was asking all the right questions, but there was no

mistaking the look in her eye or the meaning behind it. Did she know her husband was a murderer?

"A woman named Dawn Salisbury is missing. Before she disappeared, she went to the Ophelia Albrecht Center. It's a safe-house for battered women. While she was there, Noelle recognized her. She thought she'd seen her somewhere, and she had."

"Where?"

"In the parking lot of the tennis club, talking, or I imagine it was more like arguing, with your husband."

Heidi went quiet, staring at the floor as she fiddled with her fingers.

"I believe Noelle saw Dawn arguing with Clark, and not long after, she showed up at the women's center, bruised and beaten. Noelle took her to the hospital. A doctor ran some tests, and do you know what he discovered? Dawn is pregnant."

Heidi shook her head, covering her face with her hands as tears spilled down her cheeks.

"When Dawn went missing, Noelle tried to find her, but she was not successful," I said. "I'm guessing she confronted Clark, accusing him of battery. Before she could go to the police, she was murdered. So, my question to you is … where was your husband on the night Noelle threw Zoey's engagement party?"

Heidi rubbed her hands across her face, trying to stop the tears, but they kept on coming.

"I … he was … I …"

She turned, staring down the hall.

"Where's Clark?" I asked. "It's all right. You can tell me."

As she raised a shaky finger, Clark stepped into the room, gun in hand.

"Heidi, go to the bedroom and close the door," he said.

"But Clark …"

"Do it—*now*!"

"No, Clark. It's time for all this madness to stop."

"What are you talking about?"

"I know about Dawn," Heidi said. "She came to see me."

"When?"

"It doesn't matter. None of it matters anymore."

"Go ahead, tell her," he said. "Tell the detective I was with you on the night of Noelle's murder. Tell her so she can leave, and we can get on with our lives."

"Leave?" I asked. "The gun in your hand suggests otherwise."

"The gun is for *our* protection. You're in my house, accusing me of things I didn't do. I have no choice but to protect myself."

"And I have no choice but to protect myself. But first, why don't you make things easier on me. Give me a confession and tell me where I can find Dawn."

"I don't know where you can find Dawn. How would I?"

"But you do know her?"

"No … I … you … stop putting words in my mouth." He glanced at Heidi. "Honey, do what I asked, okay? Tell her we were together. She's got the wrong guy."

"No, Clark," Heidi said. "I won't tell her … because it would be a lie, and I'm tired of all the lies. You were gone that night. You came home just after midnight. I know because you came up to our room to make sure I was sleeping. You leaned over, gave me a kiss, and then you stripped down, went outside, and … I … I watched you burn the clothes you were wearing in the firepit in the backyard. But they didn't burn, not all the way. If anything happens to me, or the detective, the glove goes straight to the police."

Clark bent down, scowling as he said, "How could you do this to me … to *us*?!"

"There is no us!" Heidi said. "Not anymore."

"Then you've left me no choice."

He raised the gun, aiming it in our direction, and I reached out, grabbing her hand and saying, "Trust me, Heidi. It's going to be okay."

Clark cackled a laugh. "It's not going to be okay. Not for *you*."

As he steadied his aim, Giovanni stepped into the room, firing his own weapon, the bullet cracking through Clark's hand. As Clark screamed in pain, he dropped his gun, and I lunged forward, picking it up.

"Oh, I'd say things are going to be just fine for us, but not for you. By the way, I want my handbag back. And one more thing, this conversation we just had? It's all on tape."

CHAPTER 36

Giovanni slung an arm around me, and the two of us watched as Whitlock stuffed a handcuffed Clark into the back of a squad car. The detective turned, offering me a thumbs-up as he smacked the top of the car, giving the officers the green light to head out. Inside the house, Heidi had been talking to Foley for some time.

When Foley emerged, he walked over and patted me on the shoulder. "You should speak with Heidi. There's something she needs to tell you."

I nodded and headed back into the house. She was on the couch, wiping a few tears from her eyes. I sat beside her. "Hey, are you doing all right?"

"I doubt I'll ever be all right. He was the love of my life, you know? That's why I protected him. And I'm sorry. I know I shouldn't have. I know it was wrong."

"We do crazy things for love sometimes."

"Yeah, but allowing Clark to get away with murder shouldn't have been one of them."

"Chief Foley said you wanted to tell me something?" I asked.

"Yes, and I want to give you something."

She handed me a slip of paper, which was folded in half. I opened it, finding an address inside.

"What's this?"

"It's where you'll find Dawn Salisbury."

Of all the things I might have expected her to say, this wasn't it.

"I don't understand," I said.

"Dawn came to me the day she left the women's center. I'd suspected Clark was cheating, but I didn't know who with or how long it had been happening."

"How did it start?"

"Dawn worked as a waitress at a diner. One night, when I was out of town visiting my mother, he went to the diner. They met and hit it off. She said he didn't have a wedding ring on his finger, and he told her he was single."

"Did you believe her?"

"I did. They started an affair, but he was careful to be discreet. They stayed at a hotel an hour away in Oceano."

"Didn't you wonder where he was when he didn't come home on time?"

"I did, but his excuses always sounded believable, everything from being away for some tennis event to fishing with friends on the weekend."

"What else did Dawn say when she came to you?"

"When she found out she was pregnant, she texted Clark, saying she needed to speak to him right away. He didn't text back for a couple of days, so she showed up at the tennis club. It infuriated him."

"I can imagine."

"She told him about the pregnancy, and that's when he admitted he was married and that they had no future together. He asked her to abort the baby. She said no."

"I'm guessing that led to the assault?"

"It did."

"And then?"

"She told me she feared for her life, and for the life of her baby. She said she had no family—no one she could rely on, anyway. So, we came up with a plan."

"What was the plan?"

"The address I just gave you … my uncle has a cabin that sits empty for most of the year. It's a couple of hours from here, and he's always said I can go there anytime I want. He even gave me a key. We decided Dawn would stay there until we figured something else out. It was never supposed to go on this long, but when Noelle was murdered, I panicked. I never wanted to believe Clark was capable of killing anyone. I still don't."

I breathed a sigh of relief. "What you've done for Dawn, a woman you don't even know, is amazing. She's alive because of you."

"I just wish I would have talked with the police earlier. I was so afraid of what would happen if they didn't believe me."

"They believe you now, and because of you, Dawn and her baby are safe."

"Isn't it weird how things work out sometimes? A woman I didn't even know, who'd been having an affair with my husband, has now become my friend."

"I think it's a beautiful thing, and I thank you for sharing your story with me."

I stood, saying goodbye and walking outside, where Giovanni was waiting for me. He pulled me in close, planting a kiss on my forehead.

"Your case has been solved," he said. "What's next?"

"Next we're going to put it all behind us because we have something far more important to do."

His eyebrows shot up. "Oh?"

"Yes, oh," I said, nudging him. "*We* have a wedding to plan."

THE END

Thank you for reading Little Hidden Fears, book 11 in the *USA Today* bestselling Georgiana Germaine mystery series.

I hope you enjoyed getting to know the characters in this story as much as I have enjoyed writing them for you. This is a continuing series with more books coming before and after the one you just read. You can find the series order (as of the date of this printing) in the "Books by Cheryl Bradshaw" section below.

In Little Dark Deeds, book 12 in the series:

It's Georgiana Germaine's wedding day. But when one of her closest friends is noticeably absent from the ceremony, Georgiana discovers a dark truth, and she soon learns her friend's life is in grave danger.

* * *

Want a sneak peek? Here's an exclusive look at chapter one …

LITTLE DARK DEEDS

LITTLE DARK DEEDS
CHAPTER 1

Tiffany Wheeler rushed around the walk-in closet, yanking clothes off hangers and stuffing them into her suitcase. One quick glance at the clock on the bedroom wall and she sighed. She was running behind. If she was going to make it to the airport in time to catch her flight to New York City, she had to be out the door in the next forty-five minutes, and she hadn't even showered yet.

Grabbing her terry-cloth bathrobe off the end of the bed, Tiffany headed for the bathroom, turning the shower's handle as she stepped inside. The cool water splashed onto her back, and she winced, wishing she'd allowed the water temperature to heat up first. But today, time was not on her side.

Tiffany reached for the soap, her thoughts turning to tomorrow and the wedding of one of her closest friends, Georgiana Germaine. Tiffany had known Georgiana since elementary school, though they'd had a rocky start. One day in the school cafeteria, Tiffany noticed a bag of Cheetos inside Georgiana's A-Team lunchbox, and she snatched it, thinking no one had seen the dirty deed. But two boys at the opposite end of the table had, and when Georgiana accused them of thievery, they were quick to point fingers, singling out the offender.

As Tiffany tried making a run for it, Georgiana sprinted in her direction, hands fisted. She punched Tiffany square in the nose, breaking it. Blood sprayed all over Tiffany's pastel pink dress, and it wasn't long before every eye in the room was on them. From then on, many of her fellow classmates called her Squirt, and Georgiana became her sworn enemy.

Years passed before Tiffany and Georgiana spoke again, when one day Georgiana found Tiffany hiding under the bleachers, mourning the traumatic breakup with her boyfriend. She'd indulged in a bit too much tequila, which had been supplied by a friend, and was far from sober. Knowing Tiffany was in no condition to go home, Georgiana decided to call Tiffany's mother and pretend she needed help on a school project. The plan worked, and for the next several hours Tiffany rested in Georgiana's bedroom, chugging water until she was sober enough to head home.

Ever since, the duo had been the best of friends.

Thinking back on it now, Tiffany laughed. Life could be crazy, but at times it had a way of mending hearts—hers and Georgiana's, at least. As happy as Tiffany was for Georgiana's upcoming nuptials, Tiffany's own love life was in shambles. One week earlier, while in the office at her law firm, a woman came in, bursting into tears the moment they made eye contact. The woman's name was Jana, and she'd come to deliver a terrible truth. Spencer, the man Tiffany had been dating for over six months, was married—*to Jana.*

Tiffany had spent the past several days grieving the breakup, her heart in pieces. The man she thought was different than the rest, a man she hoped to one day marry, had been fooling her all along, and she'd fallen for it.

Again.

It wasn't an ideal time for her to be attending a wedding.

But tomorrow wasn't about her.

It was about Georgiana.

And she was determined to push her feelings of discomfort to the side and put on a happy face for her dear friend.

Returning to the present moment, Tiffany reached for the shampoo. Popping the lid open, she squirted a dollop onto her palm, then rubbed her hands together to create a thick lather. She worked it into her long, blond hair, and as the suds fell over her face, she heard what sounded like a door closing. Through the muffled sound of the water, she couldn't be sure.

She rinsed the suds out of her eyes, moved the shower curtain to the side, and peeked out, listening.

A breeze drifted by. She guessed it was from the window she'd left open in the bedroom. It had been a windy day—perhaps the wind had blown something over.

Deciding it was nothing, Tiffany shrugged, dipping beneath the water for one last rinse. She shut the water off and stepped out, bending down to reach for her bathrobe, which had fallen on the floor. She wrapped it around herself and turned, panic flooding her mind as she came to the realization she was not alone.

An intruder stood in the bathroom's doorway, knife in hand.

With no way to escape, she stepped back. "No, please. Don't hurt me."

Her pleas for mercy fell on deaf ears, the knife lifting and then plunging down—again, and again, and again.

As Tiffany drew her last breaths, one last thought ran through her mind—if Georgiana would have been in her position, what would she have done?

* * *

I hope you enjoyed the sneak peek!

Reserve your copy of Little Dark Deeds today at CherylBradshawStore.Com (it's sure appreciated when you buy direct from the store).

ENJOY HIDDEN FEARS?

You can show your appreciation by leaving a review on Amazon, Barnes & Noble, Apple Books, Google Play, Kobo, or Goodreads.

If you write a review, please be sure to email Cheryl (cheryl@authorcherylbradshaw.com) so she can express her gratitude. She does her best to reply to as many emails as she can, and she appreciates every piece of mail she receives.

About Cheryl Bradshaw

Cheryl Bradshaw is a New York Times and 11-time USA Today bestselling author writing in multiple genres, including mystery, thriller, romantic suspense, supernatural suspense, and poetry. She is a Shamus Award finalist for best private eye novel of the year, an eFestival of Words winner for best thriller, and has published over fifty books since 2011.
When she's not writing, Cheryl loves jet-setting to new countries, playing with her grandkids, high tea, and pursuing a wishful side career as a professional food tester of wine and cheese.

* * *

Never Miss One of Cheryl's Book's Again!

Sign up for Cheryl Bradshaw's "Killer Newsletter" today to be the first to know when a new book is released and to enter to win fun bookish swag. You'll also receive some fantastic book freebies just for joining!

Learn more by visiting CherylBradshawStore.Com

BOOKS BY CHERYL BRADSHAW

Sloane Monroe Series

Silent as the Grave (Prequel, Book 0)

When the body of Rebecca Barlow is found floating in the lake, private investigator Sloane Monroe takes on her very first homicide.

Black Diamond Death (Book 1)

Charlotte Halliwell has a secret. But before revealing it to her sister, she's found dead.

Murder in Mind (Book 2)

A woman is found murdered, the serial killer's trademark "S" carved into her wrist.

I Have a Secret (Book 3)

Doug Ward has been running from his past for twenty years. But after his fourth whisky of the night, he doesn't want to keep quiet, not anymore.

Stranger in Town (Book 4)

A frantic mother runs down the aisles, searching for her missing daughter. But little Olivia is already gone.

Bed of Bones (Book 5) (USA Today Bestselling Book)

Sometimes even the deepest, darkest secrets find their way to the surface.

Flirting with Danger (Book 5.5) A Sloane Monroe Short Story

A fancy hotel. A weekend getaway. For Sloane Monroe, rest has finally arrived, until the lights go out, a woman screams, and Sloane's nightmare begins.

Hush Now Baby (Book 6) (USA Today Bestselling Book)

Serena Westwood tiptoes to her baby's crib and looks inside, startled to find her newborn son is gone.

Dead of Night (Book 6.5) A Sloane Monroe Short Story

After her mother-in-law is fatally stabbed, Wren is seen fleeing with the bloody knife. Is Wren the killer, or is a dark, scandalous family secret to blame?

Gone Daddy Gone (Book 7) (USA Today Bestselling Book)

A man lurks behind Shelby in the park. Who is he? And why does he have a gun?

Smoke & Mirrors (Book 8) (USA Today Bestselling Book)

Grace Ashby wakes to the sound of a horrifying scream. She races down the hallway, finding her mother's lifeless body on the floor in a pool of blood. Her mother's boyfriend Hugh is hunched over her, but is Hugh really her mother's killer?

Sloane Monroe Stories: Deadly Sins

Deadly Sins: Sloth (Book 1)

Darryl has been shot, and a mysterious woman is sprawled out on the floor in his hallway. She's dead too. Who is she? And why have they both been murdered?

Deadly Sins: Wrath (Book 2)

Headlights flash through Maddie's car's back windshield, someone following close behind. When her car careens into a nearby tree, the chase comes to an end. But for Maddie, the end is just the beginning.

Deadly Sins: Lust (Book 3)

Marissa Calhoun sits alone on a beach-like swimming hole nestled on Australia's foreshore. Tonight, the lagoon is hers and hers alone. Or is it?

Deadly Sins: Greed (Book 4)

It was just another day for mob boss Giovanni Luciana until he took his car for a drive.

Deadly Sins: Envy (Book 5)

A cryptic message. A missing niece. And only twenty-four hours to pay.

Deadly Sins: Pride (Book 6)

A secret lies within the Kingston mansion's walls, a secret that's about to
bring the past into the present.

Sloane & Maddie, Peril Awaits (Co-Authored with Janet Fix)

The Silent Boy (Book 1)

*In the hallway of a local tavern, six-year-old Louie Alvarez waits for his mother
to take him home. A scream rips through the air, followed by the sound of a gun
being fired. Louie freezes, then turns, with a single thought on his mind: RUN.*

The Shadow Children (Book 2)

*Within the tunnels of the historic port city of Savannah, fourteen-year-old Andi
Leland has her mind set on freedom—not just for herself but for all the other
teens who have come before her.*

The Broken Soul (Book 3)

*When the party of a lifetime becomes a party to the death, the lines become
blurred. Friends become enemies. Drugs become weapons. And that's just the
beginning.*

The Widow Maker (Book 4)

*A friend murdered. A business in trouble. A marriage struggling to survive. And
that's just the beginning.*

Georgiana Germaine Series

Little Girl Lost (Book 1)

*For the past two years, former detective Georgiana "Gigi" Germaine has been
living off the grid, until today, when she hears some disturbing news that
shakes her.*

Little Lost Secrets (Book 2)

When bones are discovered inside the walls during a home renovation, Georgiana uncovers a secret that's linked to her father's untimely death thirty years earlier.

Little Broken Things (Book 3)

Twenty-year-old Olivia Spencer sits at her desk in her mother's bookshop, dreaming about her upcoming wedding. The store may be closed, but she's not alone, and her dream is about to become her worst nightmare.

Little White Lies (Book 4)

When a serial killer sweeps through the streets of Cambria, California, Georgiana Germaine gets swept up into a tangled web of deception and lies.

Little Tangled Webs (Book 5)

What if you knew the person you loved was murdered, but no one else believed you? Eighteen-year-old Harper Ellis knows she's right, and she's prepared to risk her life to prove it.

Little Shattered Dreams (Book 6)

At fifty-five, Quinn Abernathy has been through her fair share of experiences in life. And tonight, her past is coming back to haunt her.

Little Last Words (Book 7)

After living in a verbally abusive relationship for the past six years, twenty-seven-year-old Penelope Barlow has finally found the courage to leave. But can she escape ... with her life?

Little Buried Secrets (Book 8)

In a split-second, a car collides with Margot, and she finds herself hurdling through the air, her bike going one way as she goes the other. Her mind whirls in this moment, as she thinks about her life and just how much she doesn't want to die.

Little Stolen Memories (Book 9)

In a secluded cabin deep within the woods, an ominous stranger is about to change the lives of six unsuspecting teenagers forever.

Little Empty Promises (Book 10)

As librarian Cordelia Bennett prepares to lock up for the night, a mysterious sound startles her. She turns. The fading light reveals a chilling presence in the shadows, and Cordelia realizes she's not alone.

Little Hidden Fears (Book 11)

Noelle Winters has just thrown the perfect engagement party ... or so she believes. As the evening winds down and the toast is about the commence, the lights go out. And for someone, the night has just turned deadly.

Addison Lockhart Series

Grayson Manor Haunting (Book 1)

When Addison Lockhart inherits Grayson Manor after her mother's untimely death, she unlocks a secret that's been kept hidden for over fifty years.

Rosecliff Manor Haunting (Book 2)

Addison Lockhart jolts awake. The dream had seemed so real. Eleven-year-old twins Vivian and Grace were so full of life, but they couldn't be. They've been dead for over forty years.

Blackthorn Manor Haunting (Book 3)

Addison Lockhart leans over the manor's window, gasping when she feels a hand on her back. She grabs the windowsill to brace herself, but it's too late-- she's already falling.

Belle Manor Haunting (Book 4)

A vehicle barrels through the stop sign, slamming into the car Addison Lockhart is inside before fleeing the scene. Who is the driver of the other car? And what secrets within the walls of Belle Manor will provide the answer?

Crawley Manor Haunting (Book 5)

Something evil is coming. Something dark. Something seeking to destroy everything and everyone in its path. And Addison Lockhart is the only one who can stop it.

Till Death do us Part Novella Series

Whispers of Murder (Book 1)

It was Isabelle Donnelly's wedding day, a moment in time that should have been the happiest in her life...until it ended in murder.

Echoes of Murder (Book 2)

When two women are found dead at the same wedding, medical examiner Reagan Davenport will stop at nothing to discover the identity of the killer.

Stand-Alone Novels

Eye for Revenge (USA Today Bestselling Book)

Quinn Montgomery wakes to find herself in the hospital. Her childhood best friend Evie is dead, and Evie's four-year-old son witnessed it all. Traumatized over what he saw, he hasn't spoken.

The Perfect Lie

When true-crime writer Alexandria Weston is found murdered on the last stop of her book tour, fellow writer Joss Jax steps in to investigate.

Hickory Dickory Dead (USA Today Bestselling Book)

Maisie Fezziwig wakes to a harrowing scream outside. Curious, she walks outside to investigate, and Maisie stumbles on a grisly murder that will change her life forever.

Roadkill (USA Today Bestselling Book)

Suburban housewife Juliette Granger has been living a secret life ... a life that's about to turn deadly for everyone she loves.